The Christmas Catch

Everyone deserves to feel the magic of Christmas.

Playlist

"Christmas Tree Farm" by Taylor Swift

"You're a Mean One, Mr. Grinch" by Tyler, The Creator

"All I Want for Christmas Is You" by Mariah Carey

"City Girl" by Ryan Hurd

"Wildest Dreams" by Taylor Swift

"Last Christmas" by Taylor Swift

"Outlaws Like Me" by Justin Moore

"A Nonsense Christmas" by Sabrina Carpenter

"Fishin' In The Dark " by Nitty Gritty Dirt Band

The Christmas Catch

HANNAH GRAY

Chapter 1

Stella

I STARE BLANKLY AT MY BOSS, ASSUMING THE WORDS THAT JUST CAME out of his mouth were a joke and he's going to start barking out his annoying hyena laugh at any second. Much to my surprise, it's not happening. Instead, he offers me a proud, immature smirk, indicating he's not bullshitting.

Against my will, a scowl tugs at my brows, and I pinch the bridge of my nose to hide it because if there's one thing Victor hates, it's feeling like people are laughing at him.

It's gotta go hand in hand with his little man syndrome.

"So, what you're saying, Victor, is … you want me to fly to Maine, two weeks before Christmas, arrive at the owners' property, and try to seal this deal?" I give him an *are you fucking kidding me* look while also trying to appear semi-nice. "Did I hear you correctly? Because I have to be honest with you, that seems … well, insane."

He relaxes behind his desk, putting his palms against the back of his head lazily. "That's exactly what you're going to do, Stella. And I'll tell you why."

I wait for him to explain why on earth I'm going to pack up and head to a tiny-ass town on the coast of Maine and bombard the owners right before the holidays when everyone's lives are already hectic enough. It's got to be his worst plan—ever. If he hopes to actually seal this deal, it would be better to do it at another time of the year.

Literally any other time. When people aren't stressed. Or frazzled. Or depressed.

I'm not depressed though. I just really, really hate Christmas.

"Well?" I finally utter. "Don't leave me hanging, Vic. I'm on the edge of my seat over here," I say dryly. "Let a girl know what's up."

A weird, smug, yet entertained expression covers his face, making his eyes scrunch up and his cheeks plump when he smirks. "Because I sent Lester out there earlier this year—in July. It was a terrible time because the fishermen were busy, and that meant they were cranky as hell." He stops, pointing at me. "That right there is why you're going now and not when it's mid-summer. Apparently, this time of the year, fishermen aren't able to get out to haul as much—something about the weather. I don't really know or care." He shakes his head. "Anyway, when Lester was there, he said there was a lot of single fishermen around." He wiggles his brows. "So, we knew right then that sending *him* out there was an error." He jerks his chin up, bobbing his head up and down like a fucking moron. "So, I'm sending in the big guns now."

I act like I'm looking behind me on both sides for someone else before I stare straight at him. "And I'm your big gun? Me? The same chick you usually send to handle your smallest deals? And that's not even to get the deal; it's more a paperwork thing."

"Well, you're great at paperwork, Stell," he coos. "And trust me, this one will come with a shit ton of paperwork."

When he doesn't respond to the other part of my question, I attempt to compose myself. "So, let me get this straight … because there are single fishermen and I have boobs—which, by the way, aren't even that big—and a vagina, which will be staying behind a set of panties, you're sending me to these fishermen?" I can't even believe the words coming from my lips. "Victor, you do understand that I'm not going to seduce them into selling us their land, right?"

"Well, yeah," he deadpans, and I sigh in relief until he adds, "because that would be illegal."

I pinch the bridge of my nose again, unsure of how such an absolute moron became the head honcho of this company. And then I remember, he was born with a silver spoon in his mouth, and his dad owns the whole thing. I'm quickly reminded why he's staring at me from the other side of this desk.

"So, if you aren't expecting me to seduce anyone into selling, why me?" I shrug. "Why do I have to be the one to deal with the grumpy-ass lobster fishermen?"

He wags his finger at me. "Seduce? No. But charm? Well, babe, there's nothing wrong with that."

I imagine punching him in the face, and it helps to mask my revulsion. For a second anyway. Charm is a huge part of the game of gaining properties, but I don't enjoy being talked to like I'm a piece of meat.

"Look, Stella, you know that you're beautiful, smart, and incredibly witty." He wiggles his eyebrows. "Which makes you the perfect fit for this job."

For a moment, I just stare at him until I finally relax in my seat again. "Flirting with a man who smells like bait sounds absolutely awful, but okay … I'll entertain you because I'm not afraid of a challenge."

He gives me a cocky chin jerk. "And that right there? That's why I chose you, Stell; that's why I chose you." He chuckles. "This property could be huge. I'm talking its very own boardwalk, restaurants, a resort, a golf course overlooking the ocean. Hell, maybe even some shopping centers. The possibilities are endless because it's a fuck ton of land."

He opens his desk drawer, pulls out a pile of papers, and tosses them in front of me. I look down at the photos of the land, running my fingers over the picture that shows the rugged coastline of Maine with the waves crashing against it. Even in a picture, I can somehow tell the water is freezing.

"It's *that* much land? We could do that much with it, I mean?" I ask, flipping to the next photo that shows a bunch of fishing boats, all on their moorings with the sun rising behind them. The orange hues of the sun hit the water, making it look like wavy, colored glass.

"Oh, fuck yeah, it is." He nods proudly, practically salivating at the mouth, just thinking about the property. "This is well over a hundred acres. All right along the coast of Maine."

"All undeveloped?"

"Most of it," he answers. "Aside from their working waterfront and a few houses and such."

"And what makes you think they'll sell?" I continue eyeing the photos, taking in the beauty, even though it's far from anyplace I have ever lived or would ever want to live. Visit? Sure. But I'll bet their nearest Starbucks isn't within an hour. No thanks.

"Because I'm sure they've never seen the kind of money we're going to offer," he states arrogantly. "We've upped the initial number we proposed last summer. By almost double. But, you know, I had to throw out something low first because you never know who's going to take it."

Letting my eyes skim the paper, I inhale sharply and blow it out. "Well, all right then. Maine … here I come." As I mutter the words, I realize this isn't like other jobs I've done.

Normally, I am more the one who goes in and finalizes the deal once it's secured. And even then, I don't typically have to travel this far.

One thing's for sure: Victor must really think this land is a gold mine. If not, he wouldn't be wasting his time.

Or mine.

Ridge

"That's the last of them, Cap," Connor calls to me, releasing the crate into the air and watching the lift pull it to the dock.

His hat's cocked sideways, just like it has been for all the years he's been on the stern of my boat. He's about my age, but he acts like he's sixteen, not twenty-eight.

"I don't call that too bad of a day, Ridge," Jake says, reaching for the strap of his oil pants.

"We still gotta dip bait, dipshit," I utter, pointing to his shoulder. "Don't be rushing out of here like your ass is on fire."

"Fuck, I forgot."

He lets a huff out, almost as if telling me that keeping him here for an extra fifteen minutes to get our bait ready for tomorrow is ruining his entire life. Too bad for him. I don't give a shit. He's worked for me for four years now, so he should know that much.

Turning to Connor as he makes his way toward us, he tips his chin up. "We gotta fuck with bait."

Connor grins, shaking his head because he actually remembered. In his defense, he's been with me since I was eighteen years old, so for ten years, he's had to deal with my shit. I like my boat to sparkle, and I prefer to have my stuff for haul ready the day before.

"Quit pouting," I grumble. "This is the first we've even been out in eight days because of the fucking wind. I'm glad you enjoyed your time off, doing whatever the fuck it is you do, but now it's time to get back to work."

"What he said," Connor agrees with a wink at Jake.

Stepping onto the side of the boat, Connor climbs up onto the wharf with Jake eventually following behind.

Half the time, my two guys fight like cats and dogs; the other half, they laugh their asses off together. And ninety-nine percent of the time, they are the biggest pains in my ass. But help is hard to find, and they are damn good workers. And both of them grew up around the ocean, so that's helpful when we're hauling through gear.

While I wait for the two of them to dip the bait so that I can load it on, I glance up at the wooded area far behind the wharf. Tucked up in the trees is my house, and about a quarter mile from mine are the houses of my parents, my brother and then my grandparents. My family has owned and operated this wharf since my dad was a kid. But I didn't just want to work at the wharf; I wanted to be on the ocean. Same with my siblings too.

I know there's a whole big world out there—shit, I go south to Florida every winter for a few months so I have the proof. But the truth is, there's no place like home. This coastline is rooted deep inside my flesh, and the waters run through my veins, giving me life. Because of that, I'll never leave.

We may not utilize every single acre we have, but I sure love how peaceful it is around here.

And when I look up on the dock at all my stacks of crates, making today my biggest haul of autumn, despite my aching back, a grin almost tugs at my lips.

Because, goddamn, it's been a good day. And now I get to go the fuck home and relax.

Chapter 2

Stella

AN EPISODE OF *THE TINDER SWINDLER* COMES TO AN END, AND I quickly hit Next, not giving a shit if the person beside me thinks I'm a creep because right now, watching a few episodes from a true crime series is the only way I'll get through this flight—even if it is under two hours.

I've never liked to fly. Something about putting a giant machine in the air after it races—really not all that fast—down the airstrip just isn't my cup of tea. At all. In fact, nothing about it seems normal to me.

The man in his sixties has attempted small talk multiple times, and while I've tried my best to be polite, this time, when I hear his voice and see him looking at me out of the corner of my eye, I ignore him and pretend like I can't hear with my headphones on. Then I remember, karma is a bitch, and what if I ignore him and then the plane goes down as a form of punishment?

Yeah. My mind went there.

And that's really not how I want to go out, if I'm being honest.

Fighting the look of irritation on my face, I pause the show and slide the headphones to my neck.

"What's that?" I ask, turning slightly toward him.

He's probably a nice guy; don't get me wrong. He seems like the type who smiles at everyone as they pass by him—opposite of me. I keep my head down, not talking unless I absolutely have to. Besides if it's for work or I'm trying to seal a deal. In those cases, I can turn the charm on real fast.

His lips turn up. "Oh, I was just asking if you're visiting Maine for the holidays or if you live there and are returning." He nods toward my phone. "Didn't mean to pull you away from your show, dear."

Yeah ... but you did.

I know that I'm a bitch for just wanting to watch my episode and be left alone. Truly, I get that. I know it's the holiday season, and everyone is feeling squishy and sentimental, and people feel like they should befriend strangers. I'd like to say my aggravation with this conversation comes from being thousands of feet in the air, but that isn't true. Not entirely anyway. I'm already not the warmest or fuzziest human. Add in being on an airplane or that it's the holiday season, and I'm downright rotten. November and December are my least favorite months of the entire year. And this dude beside me? Well, he's not really making anything better.

"I'm just visiting for a few days," I say, knowing I need to ask him the same thing but considering skipping it. Then the word *karma* flashes across my brain again. "You?" I manage to squeak out.

"I'm headed to visit my son and his family for Christmas," he answers proudly. "I fly out and stay a few weeks for Christmas every year."

His answer makes me wish I had taken the bitchy way out and not asked, but it's not his fault that part of the reason I despise this season so much is because I have no family to spend it with. I've considered getting a pet, but I always work so many hours that I know it wouldn't be fair to the poor, innocent creature that was unlucky enough to come home with me.

"That's nice." I muster up a smile—or as close to one as I can possibly offer. "Well, I hope you have a wonderful holiday."

I start to reach for my headphones, but his voice stops me.

"What part of Maine are you headed to?" he blurts out, still looking at me politely, even though I'm doing everything in my power to end this conversation. "If you don't mind me asking."

"Holiday Harbor," I mumble because even the name of the damn town is annoying. Not as annoying as another Maine place I saw that was called Christmas Cove, but still … irritating nonetheless.

"Well, I'll be. My family lives just the next town over." He chuckles. "Small world, I guess."

"Sure is," I say, attempting to flash him a smile because he seems like a nice enough man, and I feel a little guilty that this season and being in the air have me on edge so much that I don't even want to talk to him. "I hope you enjoy your Christmas with your family."

"Thank you." He pauses. "I hope you have a good trip and enjoy seeing Maine. I don't know if you've ever been there, but it's … it's truly one of a kind. It's one of those places that really sticks with you, you know?"

I don't know what he means, but I'm not going to tell him that. So, instead, I just smile, nod, and put my headphones back on. I press play on my phone, but as the documentary begins to start up again on the screen, his words keep repeating over and over again in my head.

"It's one of those places that really sticks with you."

I've bounced around between so many places, and I don't think I've ever felt like anywhere stuck with me. At least not in a positive way.

North Dakota stuck with me because that was where I was taken from my parents. Granted, it wasn't a safe environment, but still, being taken out of the only home you've ever known? Yeah, that'll stick with you. A few hours south of where I grew up, still in North Dakota, was where I went into the foster care system for the first time and figured out that I might have been better off with my parents. Even though they were addicts, they'd at least ignored me. Ohio was where I learned my mom and dad were both dead. Virginia was where one of my foster fathers came on to me when I was fifteen, forcing me to kick him in the nuts, and where I was slapped across the face from his wife because she said I'd led him on. New Jersey was where I became emancipated and moved into a small, crappy apartment. But New Jersey was also where I received a scholarship to college in New York, so I guess that's the one positive from all of the places I've been.

I moved to New York ten years ago, when I was eighteen. And now, I've become accustomed to the honking horns, fast-paced days, and lively nights. It really is the city that never sleeps, and that means it's always busy, and nothing is ever quiet. And as long as everything around me remains busy and there's noise, I don't have to stop and think about the past. I can just bury myself in work and think about the future I want.

And the first step in my future is arriving in Maine and convincing these fishermen to sell Ironbound Developments their property. If I can do that, I'll surely move up the ladder. And the faster I move up the ladder, the more my name gets out there, the more money I save, and the closer I am to starting my very own company.

It's all going to happen, thanks to these fishermen.

Maine is everything that I expected it to be. At least, so far, the hour I've spent in my rental car, driving from the airport toward this so-called promised land, has proven that it is. Trees. *A whole lot of trees.* And cars with people who enjoy driving slowly, like they are all on a Sunday drive even though it's Thursday afternoon and they should be all ready to get home from work. But if that's the case, they've got a weird way of showing it.

I've passed through a few small towns, and I haven't heard a single honking horn. No one is yelling a slew of choice words out their car window, and everything seems weirdly calm. I suppose I can see the appeal when people come here to escape. Especially if you enjoy the whole … great outdoors thing, but this isn't my cup of tea. I like busy. And the horns? They comfort me.

They are sure better than quiet.

I glance at the screen and see I only have about five minutes left of driving until I arrive at the small house the company rented for me to stay in. I looked at the pictures briefly. It's right on the ocean, and it sits on land that borders the hundreds of acres Ironbound is trying to acquire. Which means the fishermen won't be able to escape me. I'll be *right* up their asses.

I think back to watching the man who had sat next to me on the plane be greeted by his family when he walked into the airport after we landed. His son, daughter-in-law, and their three kids all looked ecstatic that they had his company for the holidays.

I should have been nicer to him.

He was obviously a stand-up guy. And yet all I could do was answer just enough of his questions so that he'd leave me alone.

Google Maps tells me to turn right in five hundred feet on Shore's Edge Drive. I narrow my eyes, taking in the row of mailboxes ahead, realizing that's exactly where I'll be turning.

When I reach the driveway, I slowly turn, glancing down the road and taking in the huge sign with a picture of a lobster at the top. Squinting, I read the lettering.

"Adams Lobster Co." I whisper the name, knowing it's the family whose land I'm here to make an offer on. "Found you."

I'm not going over there today though. No, today has been long enough, and all I want to do is drop my stuff off, make sure the house is clean enough to stay in and not crawling with mice or spiders or whatever else Maine may be full of, and then find the nearest grocery store and stock up on everything I'll need for the week.

Tomorrow. Yep, that's when I'll have to plaster on my sweetest smile and charm the hell out of these fishermen. But I also know that some of these fishermen could have wives or girlfriends, and that may throw a curveball in the whole thing—because we all know who the shrewd ones really are.

See, men are pretty easy to figure out. Women? Not so much.

Either way, I've always enjoyed a challenge.

Chapter 3

Ridge

"HELLO?" MY MOM ANSWERS THE PHONE, AND HER VOICE PLAYS over the speakers in my truck as I drive toward town.

There are only a few cars out and about now that it's on the cusp of dusk, seeing as it gets dark before five o'clock these days. Everyone else hates it, but for me, it makes it easier to go to bed at eight o'clock when the sun's been down for hours anyway.

"Hey," I say, pressing on the brakes as a random car pulls out in front of me, resisting the urge to swear for the sole reason my mother is on the other line. Not like she'd think much of it. She raised four boys after all. "I'm headed to the store. Just checking if you guys need anything."

"Oh, well . . ." She pauses. "No, no. It's all right. I can run over to town tomorrow."

"What is it?" I drawl slowly. "Or text me a list if it's more than three things. You know my memory sucks."

"Okay, as long as you're sure," she chirps. "I could use some bagels and cream cheese. We ran out, and your dad is going to haul in the morning, and you know how he gets when he doesn't get to eat his normal breakfast. And if you want to grab a jug of that iced coffee stuff he likes—he's really into that now that your brother had him try it."

"That's all shit for Dad," I utter. "What about you? Don't you need anything? You're the one who's been helping me with my logbook when I screw it up."

And thank fuck she has because with these new laws and regulations in place, there's no room for error. So, logging my catch every time I go to haul has to be done, and I fucking hate doing it. My mom though? That poor woman has to do it for my dad and all of us moronic kids.

"Well, yeah, but I do it for your brothers too." She laughs. "The only thing I need is another package of garlic bread to go with the lasagna to-night. I swore I got some, but I can't find it."

"So, garlic bread, bagels, cream cheese, and a jug of Dad's iced coffee that he seems to think is so great." I cringe. "That's four things. Hopefully, I can remember it all."

"If not, it's fine," she says. "And you know, that iced coffee really isn't that bad. I tried it, and it's pretty good with that caramel creamer he gets," she says. "But anyway, thanks for grabbing all of that, babe."

"No problem." I pause. "Got room for one more for dinner? I don't feel like cooking."

"Well, of course," she says without hesitation.

If my mom could have it her way, we'd all come to dinner every night. Although, I'd say, most nights, she's got at least one of us—if not more.

"Easton is coming over, too, since it's his favorite meal and all. But in that case, why don't you grab *two* packs of garlic bread instead?"

"Ohhh, so you invited East before me?" I drawl. "I see how it is. Baby brother got the invite, and I had to invite myself. Bet he didn't even go to the store and ask what you guys needed to get included, did he?" I tease her, knowing she'll get all flustered because my mom constantly tries to keep everything even between us boys.

"Oh, cut it out, would ya? We'd love to have you both. Come on over."

"Be over shortly," I toss back.

"See ya in a few," she says, ending the call just as I turn into the park-ing lot of the Bold Coasts Grocery store.

For a late Thursday afternoon, it's about what I expected, with just a handful of cars in the parking lot. It's December in Eastern Edge—the county my family and I live in—and this time of the year, the only people around are locals. In the summer, there's more out-of-state license plates, but right now, no one wants to visit New England.

Well, no one in their right mind anyway.

When I park next to a small SUV, I instantly recognize it as the car that pulled out in front of me, and I shake my head. Grabbing my ball cap from the dashboard, I pull it down onto my head before jumping out of the truck.

"Sweet truck, Ridge," a teenager I've seen around town says, eyeing over my new truck. I can't think of his name, but I know his mom and dad. "Is that a Denali?"

I grimace internally, trying my best to hide it from him. This kid is genuinely excited because he clearly likes trucks. I got this one because it was my favorite, but I feel like a major douche, saying the word *Denali* out loud, like that's supposed to make me cool or something.

So, instead, I just give him a nod. "It is."

"Wow … it looks sick, man." He looks my truck all over. "Holy shit, it's an Ultimate? That's badass. I can't wait till I get my own boat so I can buy a truck like this."

I'm uncomfortable as fuck, and I don't have a clue what to say.

Lobster fishing has its good times, sure. And despite what people may think, it's granted me far more than I ever thought possible. But it's also stressful as hell. And with the ever-changing rules and guidelines that are always being implemented, I don't know how many more years of solid fishing there are in front of us. Not to mention, my entire family also owns and operates a wharf, and when we aren't on our own boats, we're tending to other fishermen who sell their lobsters to our pound.

So, instead of telling him to think long and hard before jumping into this industry because it's not all it's cracked up to be some days, I just flash him a smile and bob my head up and down. "Thanks, man. Have a good rest of your day."

"You too, Ridge." He answers like we're old friends, giving me a wave.

Don't get me wrong; I want to see young fishermen come up and make a go of it in the fishing industry because that's the only way we'll keep the fishery going. But they can't only want to do it because they look at what some of the more established fishermen have and want that for themselves. They have to do it because they genuinely love working on the water. Which I can say with my entire soul that I do. On the Atlantic is where I feel most at home.

I walk through the automatic doors, instantly feeling the warmth of the heat after being outside in twenty-degree air. Christmas music plays faintly through the extremely decorated store—because one thing this town loves is the holidays.

Reaching for a basket, I head toward the produce first to get myself some apples and bananas. I don't need much today, just some shit to throw in my lunch box for tomorrow. I planned to get stuff to make a sandwich, but now that I've invited myself to my parents' for dinner, I'll for sure be taking some of that lasagna to heat up instead. My dad makes fun of me and my brothers for having microwaves on our boats, but I bet he won't be laughing tomorrow when he's forcing down his ham and cheese sandwich and we're all eating hot lasagna.

I put some apples into a bag and drop them into my basket before heading toward the bananas, but just as I go to reach for a bundle, someone's hand bumps mine, and I look up into the prettiest hazel eyes I've ever seen.

"Sorry," she says, pulling her hand back and lifting her other one that's holding a piece of paper. "I was looking down at my list and not paying attention."

"No big deal," I drawl, grabbing a bundle of bananas and stepping back while keeping my gaze on her.

She doesn't look like she's from around here, and if she were ... I would have known about her before now.

Her brownish-red hair falls past her shoulders in big waves and has this sort of shine to it. Her skin is porcelain, but her cheeks have a hint of red in them, and I don't know if it's from our hands touching, the cold air outside, or makeup.

"Well, I'll just ..." She bites down on her bottom lip, grabbing a bundle and throwing them into her basket. "Have a good day."

She turns away from me, and my eyes involuntarily fall to her ass and then her legs. I've always been an ass and legs man—I like something I can hold on to. And she sure as fuck has that.

Shaking my head, I focus my eyes on the back of her head, not wanting to be a pervert when I've only exchanged a few words with the woman. I need to be respectful.

I open my mouth to ask her where she's visiting from, but I'm stopped quickly.

"Hey, Ridge," a voice says, followed by a giggle.

For a moment, my eyes stay on the redhead until she rounds the corner and falls out of sight. Slowly, I turn around to find two girls from in town, smiling at me. They can't be much more than eighteen, and at twenty-eight, I'm not interested.

"Hey," I say, smiling but then turning away from them.

It may seem rude, but I can't seem too friendly. Both of their dads sell their lobsters to my family's pound, and I don't want to come off as a creeper.

"Ugh, he's so hot," one of them whispers. "One night. That's literally all I want."

"One night? I'd want, like … twenty," the other adds. "He's straight-up freaking sexy."

"Even his boat's name is hot." Her voice grows smaller, the farther away I get. "*Eastern Outlaw … even saying it makes me squirm in need.*"

I don't know whether to be flattered or mortified. Either way, I just keep walking and head toward the next aisle to get the hell out of here.

Teenage girls who giggle and turn red when they talk to me are nothing I'm interested in, so even if they are of age, I don't care. I've had my fun with sleeping around, and sure, I'll still bring a woman home now and then and show her a good time, but all of that just doesn't sound interesting anymore. In fact, it's pretty fucking old.

Wow. Is this what it's like to grow up?

Fuck, I hope not.

Stella

Who would have thought that this sleepy little town in Maine would have such delicious eye candy? And that's exactly what the dude at the banana rack was. Delicious eye candy. And did I fight back a growl when he grabbed the bananas? Yes. Yes, I did.

He probably has a big banana.

Jesus Christ, what is wrong with me? I'm here on a business trip. I don't have time to be thinking about some random guy's banana.

Besides, just because he was a big, muscular man doesn't mean he's packing a large banana anyway. It could be more like one of those tiny ones. I'm not even quite sure of their real purpose. You can't really eat them. I mean, they are cute and everything, but that's all.

All right, seriously, enough with the bananas.

I grab the rest of the items on my list in a hurry, not wanting to run into him again because, clearly, I'm not thinking straight right now, and I head to the register.

I'm a little surprised when I walk up to the registers to find most of them are self-checkout. I guess I assumed that in a town this small, there would only be real grocery clerks checking people out, but I'm thankful to learn I was wrong because self-checkout is my jam.

From the corner of my eye, I see *him* approaching. My back grows hot, and I scurry to scan the last few items I have in my basket. Once I have, I insert my card and enter my PIN.

As the machine takes its slow-ass time to work, I glance sideways at Banana Man as he scans his own things, noticing that he doesn't have that much. He wears jeans, Nike sneakers, and a blue hoodie. All paired with a Boston Red Sox hat, which instantly has my nose scrunching because I'm a die-hard Yankees fan.

The machine makes a beeping sound. When I look at the screen, I frown at the words *Card Declined*, and the back of my neck begins to sweat. I know there's plenty of money in my account, but sometimes, when I'm traveling, the stupid bank thinks my charges are fraud, and they turn my card off.

Damn those precautionary fuckers, making me look like a loser right now. In the past, I had plenty of times when I really didn't have any money in my account so my card got declined, but right now? I know for a fact that there is money in there, so this is annoying as hell.

Scrambling, I dig in my purse, but all I have is a few one-dollar bills and a five. I had a credit card, but I paid it off and canceled it a few months ago, and right about now, I'm regretting that very adult-like decision.

Pulling out my phone, I decide to call my bank. It should be open for another seven minutes, and hopefully, I can get this all squared away.

"Ma'am, is everything okay with the machine?" a man who works here asks, stepping beside me.

"Oh, um, yes." My cheeks burn. "I am traveling, and my bank turned my card off, thinking the out-of-state charges were fraud." I press the number one on my screen to speak to a representative and hold my phone up to the man. "Just getting it sorted out now."

I hear a woman's voice, but then the line cuts in and out, making it impossible to understand her.

"Hi, I am on a business trip in Maine, and my card isn't working," I say as quietly as I can, knowing sexy Banana Man is five feet from me. "Hello?"

Crickets. That's what I hear on the other end. Fucking crickets just before the line goes completely dead and the call ends.

I attempt to call back, but I can't even get it to ring because the service in this store is so shitty.

"Hey," I say to the worker now that he's stepped away. "I need to call my bank to get my card fixed. I'll be right back inside to pay for this. Can I leave it here?"

He looks around. "Well, it's kind of in the way for the other customers."

I swing my gaze around, my lips forming a flat line. "The other three? Yeah … I think they'll be okay, seeing as there are six registers here"—I glance at his name tag—"Rob."

I don't wait for him to reply before I bolt toward the doors, hoping that I'll have more service outside. The cold air hits me in the face, and it's not long before my teeth are chattering as I attempt to call the bank back. But after about eight tries, I realize the service is no better by the door, and I head inside to see if I can use the landline.

When the automatic doors open, my heart skips a beat when I see Banana Man strutting toward me. He gives me a tiny grin, exposing a dimple, and I think my thighs might actually clench.

He extends his arm, holding a bag out to me. "Here's your stuff. Hope it's okay that I put it all in one bag." He stops. "Well, I put your Toaster Strudels in a separate one, but then stuck them in that bag to make it easier to carry for ya."

At first, I'm confused. Then, I'm charmed. Suddenly … I'm freaking annoyed. How dare he just step in and try to be my superhero!

"Um … well, why would you do that? I was going to call my bank from the landline in here," I say flatly. Embarrassed as hell that this random, very attractive stranger just bought my crap.

"I did it because the service inside here and until you're on the edge of the parking lot sucks, and since you're from out of town, I figured you didn't know that." He moves the bag closer to me. "You gonna take this or what?"

My eyes dart to the bag, and slowly, I take it from him. "Um … thanks? I guess?" I wish I could seem more thankful, but my entire life, I've been independent, and little gestures like this one make me feel like that independence is being stripped from me.

"No problem," he utters, giving me the slightest head nod. "Happy holidays."

When he turns around, heading outside, I wait an extra minute before walking to my rental car. Because right now...I do not want any more run ins with the banana man tonight.

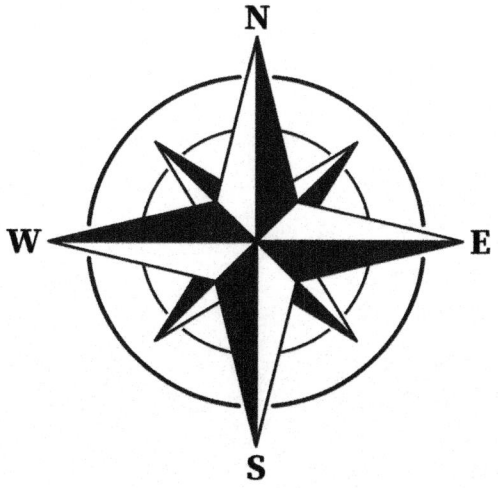

Chapter 4

Ridge

THE BOYS SEND THE LAST CRATE OF LOBSTERS UP TO THE WHARF to be weighed before turning toward me. They know I'll be here a while, but I can see it on their faces that they are more than ready to go home. It's spitting snow. It's cold. We've been out here since three this morning, and now it's five at night and dark outside again. The whole day has come and gone, and I can't blame them for being over it.

"You, uh … fixing the valves tonight, Cap? Or …" Jake says, peeling his oil pants off and throwing them on the hanger.

"Yeah, I've got to look it over to see if it's an easy fix or if it's going to drive me nuts," I mutter, looking at both of my guys. "Go on, whiny asses; get out of here. You both look like shit."

I don't have to tell them twice; they both take off like their asses are on fire before I get the chance to change my mind. Not like I would because, right now, I need some quiet.

The boat started this weird vibration early in the day, and I was scared as hell that something was going to be seriously wrong with the engine. Somehow, we limped through. But when an engine like the one on my boat has a problem, it can easily cost tens of thousands of dollars to get it straightened out—not to mention, I have to sail it a solid two hours to the closest diesel mechanic.

I switch the light down forward of my boat and make my way into the engine room to look things over. Right away, I notice something isn't quite right when I see the hoses have pissed hydraulic fuel all over the place, instantly ticking me off. Not only because I have to fix it, but because I have to clean it up too.

"Pile of fucking shit," I growl to myself because I'm tired, and the last thing I want to do is fuck with this boat right now.

The engine has given me more trouble than any other one I've ever had, but the boat itself is perfect for me because I had it built exactly like I wanted it.

"Ridge?" my dad's deep voice calls, and I'm almost grateful for another distraction before this vessel pisses me off more. "You down there, bud?"

"Yep," I call back. "Give me a second. I'll be right up."

Grabbing a rag, I wipe my hands and head toward the deck. When I walk out, my dad is standing up on the wharf under the lights we had put in a few years ago. I'm not surprised to see him—that fucker is always here. Who I am surprised to see though is … the person standing beside him.

The girl from the grocery store. The one whose card wouldn't work and she got really fucking mad when I paid for her shit.

I don't know how it's even possible, but I swear she's even prettier in the moonlight.

She may be insanely attractive, but that doesn't take away from the fact that she's downright mean. And that's not my type.

I don't have a fucking clue why she's here or why she has an iPad tucked under her arm.

"What's she doing here?" I ask bluntly.

When my dad, a man who always has the utmost respect for women, looks as irritated as I do, I know one thing for certain.

She's here for the wrong reasons.

Stella

"This is Stella. Stella, this is my son, Ridge." Mr. Adams sighs. "She came from New York and works for Ironbound Developments." He pauses. "Apparently … once again … they want to make us an offer for our land."

"Did you tell her to tell her company to fuck off?" Ridge says sharply. "Or do you need me to do that?"

"Ridge, go easy on her. She's just the messenger," his father says, keeping his tone low. "Guess they are stuck on wanting to make it into some sort of a resort with some possible shopping, among lots of other things."

"Dining too," I add, chiming in like that'll be the one thing that sells them on the idea.

I mean, this place could certainly use more food options. I think I counted one coffee shop and one restaurant, and both looked a little debatable.

"Oh, yeah ... is that right?" Banana Man drawls slowly and calculatedly, totally ignoring my comment about dining because he obviously doesn't give a shit about getting a nice meal outside of his home.

The six-feet-three, maybe six-four, man beside me, who has to be in his fifties, is annoyed, and it's more than obvious. But now, his son, who stands as tall as he does, somehow looks even more pissed than his father.

"It appears so," Mr. Adams drawls, suddenly seeming relaxed, and I have a feeling it's because he knows his son's going to handle this situation for him.

Ridge puts his foot on the side of his boat and looks up at me with nothing but pure animosity in his eyes. "I hate to break it to you, Fireball, but this land ain't for sale."

Ain't isn't a word, douchebag, and my name isn't Fireball, either. That's what I want to say, but I know it's not an option.

I came here to do one job—get this land. It's obvious that even though the land is in the father, Mathew's, name ... the guy standing on the boat, smirking up at me, is the alpha when it comes to this property. If I want the land, I'll need to go through him first.

Not literally or anything ... even if he is really, really hot.

I keep my iPad tucked under my arm for a moment before, finally, I haul it out and bring up the image of a mock-up of the completed project. "As you can see here, you'd really be doing a service to your community, Mr. Adams." I direct my voice at the younger dude, but every now and then, I flash my eyes to his dad as well. "And the best part of it is, you could keep the land your wharf sits on because, to be honest, the wharf and all the boats coming and going make it that much more desirable."

"And what, Fireball, you want us to live on our boats because you want the land our houses are on?" he tosses back, eyes becoming damn near slits. "Sorry that you brought your fancy self with your expensive, ugly-ass shoes and designer clothing all the way to Eastern Edge, but we're not interested in anything you've got to say."

My gaze narrows, and I have to fight to not look down at my feet. My shoes are not ugly. Though they do look designer, they actually aren't.

"Ridge—" The father opens his mouth, about to tell him he's being too harsh, but when his son's angry blue eyes dart to his, he sighs. "He's right. We aren't interested in whatever you came here for. So, tell your boss that it was a wasted trip and he ought to buy you a ticket back home."

As much as I want to keep it together, these men are striking every nerve inside of me, making it damn hard. "And why would I need to call my boss?" I tuck the iPad back under my arm and shrug. "I think I'm plenty capable of booking a flight … thanks."

"Well, of course you are," Mr. Adams says quickly. "That's not what I meant. I was just saying … since I'm guessing it's a company expense, is all."

"And who says I don't own the company, Mr. Adams?" I lift a brow.

"You don't," Ridge utters. "We've been through this quite a few times, Fireball. Let me tell you how it goes and see if it tracks. The big boss man— or woman—is always the last to come out." He looks me up and down, playing with me like I'm his prey. "First, they send the weakest one, and we met that guy this summer. Poor bastard. Couldn't sell water in a drought. Next, they send the one who's trying to climb the ladder." There's a short pause before he points at me. "And look … here you are."

Just being here and letting them know we're interested in this land has his boxers in a bunch. A big one at that. I'd like to tell him to fuck off, but that's not professional, and it's certainly not going to get me any closer to sealing this deal either.

"Tell you what. Why don't you gentlemen at least hear me out over dinner?" I smile—or I attempt to. "You can come to my Airbnb. And you are welcome to bring your wives or the rest of the family." I say the second part, hoping they'll say the others are out of town. I don't know how many other Ridge Adamses I can handle; I did my research on this family the night before I flew here, so I know that Ridge has three brothers, and I'm pretty sure they all live right around here too.

Hopefully, they're more delightful.

The men glance at each other, and even though it's obvious Ridge can hardly stand the sight of me, I get the feeling that his dad feels bad—which I hate, but I also know that I could use it to my advantage.

"I'll check with my wife, Katherine," Mr. Adams says, his voice low, like I've just put him in the worst spot ever.

"I've been out to haul all day, so tonight's not going to work," Ridge utters. "Also, we're not coming to your Airbnb," he adds, grabbing a tool out of his bag and holding it at his side. "If you want to talk, you can come to us."

I shouldn't feel hopeful, given the absolute glare that's still resting on his face. But he didn't say no, so that's got to count for something.

"All right, that sounds fine." I fake a polite smile, even though I want to punch him in the face.

"I'll talk to my brothers," he grumbles before turning his attention to his dad. "A hose blew, so I've got to repair it before it gets any later."

"Go on." Mr. Adams nods.

As Ridge makes his way back toward where he first appeared from, he spares me one more glance. His eyes are filled with humor, and a smirk tugs at his lips. "Hey, Fireball." He jerks his chin up. "If you think I'm a dick, wait till there's three more of me sitting at a table with you while you try to make your pitch."

"I live in New York City," I coo. "I work in a building full of men who think they are God's gift to earth. So, trust me, I'll be just fine. Thanks though."

I fight back my eye roll, and after another glare, he disappears back into the wheelhouse of his boat.

Reaching into my pocket, I pull out a business card and hold it out to Mr. Adams. "My cell is on there. Please, let me know a day and time that works for all of you."

Reluctantly, he takes it. "Will do," he mutters, looking down at it. "Oh, and, Stella?"

"Yeah?"

"Good luck." He cringes. "My boys? They love this land. This is their pride—their legacy." He looks at me. "So, while they may agree to hear you out … us selling? It's never going to happen."

Before I can come up with something to say, he walks off, leaving me on the wharf by myself in the cold December night air. I stand here for a second, looking around at the dimly lit cove with the lobster boats scattered throughout the water before, finally, I turn and leave before Ridge gets a chance to come back and be a dick once more.

Dick should be that guy's middle name.

Chapter 5

Ridge

"Ol' Outlaw, you on here?" comes over my radio as I sail in past the lighthouse, headed into the wharf to sell today's catch. I know it's my brother Riley's voice right away.

Like a jackass, I felt cool and named my boat *Eastern Outlaw* right after I graduated high school. Years later, I knew it made me look like a cocky prick, but my grandfather had helped me pick the name out after I got busted throwing a party when I was eighteen. So, when I got a new boat, I named it the same thing.

Picking up the microphone, I bring it closer to my face and keep my other hand on the wheel. "Yeah, go ahead," I say to Riley.

"What the fuck is this dinner bullshit tonight?"

I can feel my two stern men's eyes on me—no doubt, they're wondering what Riley is talking about. The thing with these two guys? They love to gossip a bit too much, and that's exactly how the rumor mill gets started—by hearing a sliver of information. If they hear why we have to meet this woman, they'll tell half the town we're selling out by tomorrow.

"Just some business thing—that's all." I leave my answer vague.

I know I'll have to fill him in on the truth before the actual dinner at our parents' tonight, which I will. But there's no sense in doing it now. Besides, it's Riley. He doesn't get worked up over anything, so he certainly won't about this.

What he will do is hit on Stella. And that's annoying as fuck because she's the villain. We need to treat her like one.

"Dude, I'm tired. We dipped traps today, and it fucking sucked," he whines. "Can't we do it another night?"

I roll my eyes, even though I know how bad dipping traps is. It's something we do yearly to get all the shit off our gear so that they aren't covered in mud and seaweed. But it makes a day of haul even longer because it takes forever.

"It won't take long. I have to haul tomorrow so I can't stay late either," I tell him. "You'll be all right, little bitch baby. And if not, Mom can give you some warm milk and you can pretend it's titty milk."

"Fuck off," he grumbles into the mic. "You're a dick."

"Yeah, well, wait until tonight," I grumble back. "Six o'clock, asshole. Be there."

"Fine," is all Riley replies, and I hang my mic up, knowing we're done talking now.

As I get closer to the wharf, I notice a person sitting on the porch at the Jacobs' family house. They go to Florida every November until May, and right away, I know that must be where Stella is staying.

The question is, how crazy is she? Because she has to be somewhat crazy to be sitting outside on a snow-covered porch, in twenty-three-degree weather, in winter.

In case she's watching, I make a point not to pay too much attention to her. A woman who looks that good? I'm sure she thinks she could put me under some sort of spell to give her what she's here for, but she's wrong. I don't give a fuck how pretty she is; she's wasting her time.

Continuing to sail past her, I pull into the wharf to sell. I'm dragging hard today, and I sure as hell am going to need an energy drink before this dinner tonight.

And maybe a few drinks to keep me from saying mean shit too.

Stella

I stand near the kitchen window, my hands still freezing from being outside just minutes ago, but I keep the binoculars against my face. My heart races in my chest, as if my body is trying to convince me that I'm doing something wrong.

The weirdest thing happened when I saw Ridge pull his boat into the wharf, and it just got more intense as I watched him and two guys on the back of his boat unload their crates—which I assumed held lobsters, but what do I know? My stomach began to feel the butterfly effect, and now … I'm biting down on my bottom lip while I take in the way he moves and the seemingly easy way he lifts things that I'm sure are insanely heavy while wearing his blue fishing gloves. The waterproof gear he's wearing over his pants, coming up to his chest, are no doubt covered in bait, and yet … he looks stupidly attractive in them, and I absolutely don't understand who I even am right now for thinking that.

I've always been into the men I meet at the gym, and yet watching him get a workout while working on his boat has me much more excited than seeing a gym bro lift weights on a damn bench press ever could.

He lifts his arm up, using his sweatshirt to wipe his forehead, and I begin fanning myself, even though I was just outside in the arctic air.

Why is this so hot?

I think back to the way he looked at me sweetly at the supermarket, and then my mind switches to how his eyes glared into my soul when he learned my reason for being here. He looked scary angry, and yet … thinking about it now, I have to squeeze my thighs together.

When he texted me this morning, bright and early, letting me know his parents' address and to be there at six tonight, I knew he must have gotten my number from his dad. I can't help but think I'm walking into the lion's den, but I can't run and hide because this is why I'm here.

His crewmates jump off the boat onto the wharf, and soon, he's standing behind the wheel, steering his boat toward the mooring I saw it sitting on yesterday. And if I thought him lifting heavy crates was hot, watching him climb to the bow of the boat and tie the knot? Well, that might be hotter.

And soon, he's in his skiff, steering it toward the dock.

And with my heart racing and the area between my thighs throbbing … I set the binoculars down, and I head into the bedroom. Because I'll be damned if I let this ache get in the way of my business pitch tonight. No, I'm going to take care of it right now.

So what if I'm about to touch myself to thoughts of the salty fisherman? I never saw a rule in the handbook saying that wasn't allowed.

Chapter 6

Ridge

"YOU FAILED TO MENTION THE DICKHEAD PROPERTY DEVELOPER was a *she*," my younger brother Riley mutters to me, "or that she's fucking hot as hell."

"First of all, I said asshole, not dickhead." I shrug. "And what's it matter if she's got a penis or not? She thinks she can come in here, write us a check, and take our land," I snap, keeping my voice as low as I can because we're in the kitchen, grabbing another drink, and she's only in the next room with my parents.

I don't know how, but they've somehow managed to be nice to her through the entire dinner. Of course, so far, she really hasn't brought up any master plans for the property, and instead, she's just been making small talk.

It's fucking weird.

"Yeah, but you didn't let me know that I might want to take her back to my place after you tell her to fuck off." He nudges me, taking a sip from his drink and stretching his neck back to look into the dining room. "She is fucking drop-dead gorgeous."

"Thank God Mom and Dad put me in charge of most of the decisions if they die." I look at him in disbelief. "Jesus, all she'd have to do is rub up against you, and you'd be signing our shit away."

"Among other things," he drawls. "Even though she was looking at you most of dinner, I'm not going to let that stop me from shooting my shot."

My brother struts off, making his way toward the dining room—probably right to Stella.

Riley loves women. Lots of women. He's not a player, but he likes to pass the love along more than the rest of us Adams boys do.

Five years ago, I definitely got around more than I care to these days. Now, I'm looking at my friends and seeing that a lot of them are getting married or even having kids, and I can't help but wonder if I'm doing everything wrong.

I have a big, beautiful house on the ocean. I work my ass off to have nice things. And yet I come home to an empty home every night.

The fact that Stella is here to make some stupid fucking offer on a priceless piece of land irks me and makes me hate her. But that doesn't explain why the hell I fucked my hand last night, imagining I was hate-fucking her.

It's been months since I've been laid. That's got to be the only reason why I'm even thinking about her in that way. Because even right now, looking out into the dining room and seeing her sitting at my parents' table? It annoys me. She has no right to be here, and I don't know why I fucking agreed to this.

Bringing my beer to my lips, I chug it down before tossing the bottle into the recyclable.

Enough small talk, Fireball. Let's fucking talk about why you're really here.

Stella

Here I sit, at the head of the table, surrounded by some of the hottest men I've ever seen. And unlike Ridge, they're not assholes.

Riley is a flirt. He could charm the skin off a snake, no doubt. Easton is a bit cockier than the other two, and he keeps looking down at his phone like he's checking the time. And then there's Tucker, who seems to be the shyest.

That leaves Ridge. The man who can say a million words in one short sentence because his words pack such a punch. His eyes may be bright blue, but there's a darkness inside of them that I find as terrifying as I do sexy. His boat is named *Eastern Outlaw*, and I guess that kind of fits.

In fact, I think I can tell a lot by their boat names, which I looked at this morning.

Riley's is *Gold Digger*, and next to it is a drawing of a woman in booty shorts and a crop top, holding a shovel. Easton's is *Risky Business*. Sweet, shy Tucker's boat is named after his mother, *Katherine Grace*.

Tucker is the oldest of the four boys, and just knowing he named his boat after his mother proves he's the nicest one in the bunch too. It all checks out because every time I look his way, he smiles and turns beet red.

"Stella, would you like another glass of wine?" Katherine says kindly as she gets out of her seat to refill her own glass.

I look at the glass and then back at her, knowing I shouldn't because I need to have a clear head if I'm going to talk business with them.

And by someone, I mostly mean Ridge. Or Riley, who comes on to me for the twentieth time.

"Uh, sure." I nod before I stand up. "You know what? I'll go with you."

A flash of concern crosses her face, but being the polite woman she obviously is, she covers it quickly with a smile and heads toward the kitchen.

Once we're alone, she fills both of our glasses up. "So, is this your first trip to Maine?" she asks, setting the bottle of wine down.

"It is," I answer, sipping from my glass.

This wine is really good, and I don't know why that surprises me, but it does. Then again, I was surprised when I drove in and saw how gorgeous Mr. and Mrs. Adams' house is. Whatever idea I had for the fishermen around here, I guess I was wrong.

"I hope you are enjoying it so far," she says sweetly. "I know it's been chilly out, but at least the whole town is decorated for the holidays, so that's nice."

"It sure is," I say as I almost choke on my wine.

She's not kidding there. This place looks like the North Pole. Even the grocery store was decorated with Christmas lights and holiday music blaring. For most people, that would be charming. For me, it makes me despise it.

Just like their house and all the decorations inside of it. Or the huge-ass Christmas tree in the living room, set in front of the windows that take up the whole front of the house, overlooking the water. This family loves Christmas—that's for sure.

"Well, shall we go back in and rejoin dinner?" I ask, turning toward the dining room, but her hand touches me.

"Hang on a second." She stops me in my tracks, coming in front of me.

"Look, you seem like a really nice woman. And obviously smart too." She smiles. "I don't want to come off as rude, so I hope you don't take this the wrong way." She pauses. "I understand you're here with one thing in

mind. Getting this land. And while I appreciate a hardworking woman, I
need you to understand something. Our land is priceless. And those men
in there are never going to budge on it. And besides, even if they were …
you'd still have to go through me."

I stare at her, but before I come up with something to say, she carries on.

"You are beautiful, but don't think for a second you are going to charm
your way into the heart of any of my boys and get them to sign over something that's been in their family for decades. It will never happen, Stella."

During dinner, she seemed like the sweetest lady. In fact, when Ridge
made little digs at me, she'd defend me in her own way by changing the
subject or shooting him a warning glance. I guess she's not so different
from her son after all.

"Ma'am," I whisper, "with all due respect, that's not really how I do
my job." I'm mad now, but I also see where she's coming from. If I were a
mom, I'd protect my children too. But I can't exactly tell her I was sent here
to charm her sons into selling their land. That sounds … icky. "I promise
you, I am very professional."

*So professional, in fact, that I fingered myself, thinking about your son
earlier.*

"I'm sure it isn't, but you aren't the first person to come in here and
try to take what's theirs, and you won't be the last. So, I'm sorry that you've
wasted your time coming here, but at the very least, let's enjoy the rest of
the evening before you go back to the city." Her words are sharp, but she
follows them up with a sympathetic smile before patting my arm. "Let's go
back and join the group. Yeah?"

I eye her over, as if we're in a standoff. Finally, I nod. "All right."
Just like I said, the women are the smart ones. Every. Single. Time.

It's the end of dinner. Katherine stuffed us all with one of the best home-
cooked meals I'd ever had and polished it off with chocolate chip bread
pudding and vanilla ice cream, and I think the button on my pants might
be on the verge of popping off.

I drank one too many glasses of wine, and I didn't even get to fully pitch Ironbound's offer because every single time it was brought up, Ridge or one of the other brothers would steer the conversation elsewhere or somehow change the subject.

And now my head is buzzing, and I'm going to call it a night.

"Well, I should get going," I say, keeping my voice from slurring as best as I can. "Dinner was delicious. Thank you so much for having me." I sound much friendlier with a buzz on. Maybe I should use this to my advantage more often to be more … people-y.

I need to go back to the house and regroup on where I go from here because this is going to be harder than I thought, and when I drink wine, I get flirty. And the last person I need to be flirting with is the one whose eyes have been on me the whole night.

Ridge "Banana Man" Adams.

When I stand, Riley and Ridge both push up from their seats. Easton left before dessert was served, and obviously, Tucker isn't going to do much talking.

"I'll give you a ride home," Ridge says, keeping his voice flat and unimpressed. Makes me wonder if he even has a personality.

"Hey, I'm going that way anyway," Riley adds in, his eyes twinkling with amusement. "I don't mind dropping her off, big brother."

Ridge's eyes cut to Riley's, narrowing slightly, as if sending a silent message. "I said I'd do it," he utters, almost more of a growl. His gaze shifts to me. "Ready?"

Looking from Ridge to Riley and finally Katherine, I grimace nervously because I took her words earlier as a warning to stay away from her boys. Instead of casting me a glare though, she smiles and nods subtly toward Ridge. Following her eyes, I glance at her son.

"Uh … sure," I squeak, moving toward Ridge. "Ready."

I'm sure she knows out of the two of her sons, Ridge is the least likely to let me close to him. She must really think I would use sex to get closer to her boys, but I would never. I'm a damn professional.

Never mind the alone time I had earlier …

I turn toward everyone and smile. I'm a little buzzed but doing my best to keep it together and not show it. "Thank you for inviting me to dinner." My gaze sweeps from face to face. "But FYI, don't think I missed the fact that you all shut me down every time I tried to talk business. So, we still have lots to discuss."

Mr. Adams grins, standing up and walking behind his wife's chair. Planting his palms on her shoulders, he shrugs. "Stella, you're welcome to stop in for dinner anytime." He pauses, his eyes narrowing. "But as for deals? We've got nothing to discuss with you."

For a second, I freeze. But then I realize I'm not surprised—not really anyway. But that doesn't mean I'm giving up.

Sighing, I tilt my head to the side. "Well, a girl can still hope, right?"

"Good night, Stella," Mrs. Adams says almost teasingly while smiling warmly at me. "Thanks for joining us."

And then it's time to follow Ridge outside to his truck, which means one thing . . .

We're going to be alone.

No. It means *I'm* going to be alone with a man I can't stand, who is also the man I fantasized about just yesterday. All after watching something as stupid as him lifting lobster crates.

Now, that's embarrassing.

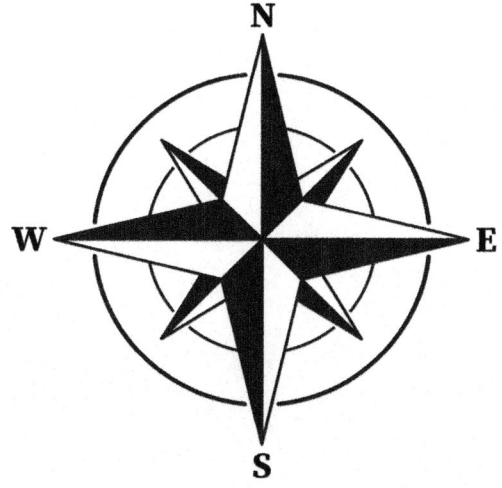

Chapter 7

Ridge

I DRIVE DOWN THE LONG DRIVEWAY TO THE HOUSE STELLA IS RENTING. And even though I can tell she's doing her best to keep her composure, trying to maintain that stick-up-her-ass thing she's got going on, it's obvious she's buzzed. And why wouldn't she be? I mean, my mom was practically refilling her wineglass every time I turned around.

She hasn't said anything to me; instead, she's just pretended to play on her phone while she sits quietly in the passenger seat of my truck. She smells fucking scrumptious, but that's the only thing about her that's sweet.

"Important business over there?" I mutter, keeping my gaze forward but still seeing the glow of her screen from the corner of my eye.

"Oh, yes," she says, doing her best not to slur. "Lots to do."

I glance at her for a split second. "If it's business, you may want to wait till the wine leaves your body, Fireball. You know, just so you don't *fumble* any deals."

When I come to a stop in front of the house, shifting my truck in park and turning toward her, she gives me a harsh glare.

"That was your plan all along, huh?" she sasses. "You wanted to get me drunk so that I couldn't make an appropriate pitch to your family." She lifts an eyebrow. "Good one, *Outlaw*."

An amused chuckle rolls from my lips at the same time my cock twitches because she used my boat name. "Sweetheart, I wasn't the one pouring wine down your throat," I muse, but suddenly, my dick hardens more when an image of me pouring other things down her throat flashes in my mind. I fight back a groan and shift around in my seat. "And if you want to know the truth, you could have drunk sparkling cider all night, had a mind sharp as glass, and it still wouldn't have mattered. We're not selling. Not now, not ever."

"Are all fishermen so *fucking* stubborn or just you?!" she hisses but then hiccups, covering her mouth. "Pretend I didn't just say that."

As much as I hate to admit it, she's kind of hot when she's pissed. Part of me wonders what would happen if I invited myself inside. Would she be offended and tell me absolutely not? Or would she be open to it, let me in, and hate-fuck me all night and make me late for haul tomorrow? Either way, I'll never know because she's drunk, and that's a big no for me.

"Sure thing, Fireball," I drawl. "Whether you're a bitch to me or sweet as pie, it won't change that you came here for no reason, and you'll have to go back to the city and return to the bottom of the ladder." I pretend to pout. "So sorry."

At first, she looks madder, but then she relaxes herself and moves her body so that she's facing me with her back to the door. A little smirk tugs at her lips, and I don't trust it one bit.

"So, what are you saying, Ridge?" she coos. "You want me to leave?"

I don't know what the fuck she's up to, but I don't trust it. Not one bit.

"Well, unless you have other people to harass about their land, then I see no reason for you to be here."

"You're so mean." She pouts. "You know that?"

She's playing me, and as much as I know that—because my bullshit radar is fucking phenomenal—my dick is still hardening as she bites down on her bottom lip, letting her teeth sink into it. She doesn't know it yet, but I'm the fucking mastermind at games, and I can play with the best of them.

"Only to you, sweetheart." I reach forward, tapping my finger to her chin and instantly watching her fight back, tensing up.

"New York is an awfully long way to come from, just to go back with absolutely nothing." I move a little closer to her and watch her breathing grow sharper through her chest. "Don't you think?"

I could kiss her, and something tells me she wouldn't fight it. In fact, the way her eyes are floating to my mouth right now, if anything, I think she'd welcome it. I'd love to find out what her lips taste like because I imagine they're sweet despite her being so damn sour. But I can't do that, especially not when she started fucking with me first just now.

"I ... I guess," she whispers nervously, suddenly looking less buzzed.

The smallest grin tugs at the corner of my mouth, and I look from her lips back to her eyes. "Maybe I should do something to make it worth your while, sweetheart. Would you like that?"

Her breathing becomes shallower, and it's more than obvious she's trying to gather herself up enough to tell me no. Before she gets the chance, I move even closer, gripping her chin to bring her face toward mine. When our lips are inches from touching, a nervous breath rushes from her just before her eyes flutter shut in anticipation. Part of me wants to close the gap and kiss her so hard that she's begging me to take her inside and fuck her brains out, but a bigger part of me gets off just on toying with her.

"Oh, Fireball …" I tsk her. "Here I thought, you were a hard-ass, yet you're practically jumping on my dick," I coo lowly, prompting her eyes to fly open. "I can't fuck you, sweetheart. After all, you're here for my family's land, and besides … you'd like that too much."

Anger replaces the desire that was on her face seconds before as her nostrils flare. She reaches between us and shoves a hand into my chest, sending me away from her.

"You, Ridge Adams, are a dick," she hisses through her teeth.

"Yeah," I say, nodding. "But you should have known that already."

As her door flies open and she hops out like her ass is on fire, I make sure she gets inside safely before I head home.

Knowing damn well that I'll be putting what just happened straight in my spank bank.

Stella

What a fucking pathetic idiot I am!

I stare at myself in the mirror, nostrils flaring because, goddammit, I'm a strong, independent woman who has always been a proud feminist. So, why in the hell did I just melt like a square of wax in a Yankee Candle melty thing when it came to a self-righteous asshole?

There's only one answer …

The wine. It had to be poisoned to make me weak. That's definitely it. It certainly wasn't his large, rough hands. Or his ocean-blue eyes. Or his deep, gravelly voice, with an accent I don't really get because it almost sounds Southern. And it's certainly not his muscled forearms because who cares about those? Pfft. Not me. Not this girl.

It's none of those things. I live in the city. I see hot, rugged men all the damn time, and I manage not to make a fool of myself. So, it must have been the wine, or maybe it's just Maine in general. Whatever it is, I need to get a handle on it. Now.

My phone vibrates in my pocket, startling me, and reluctantly, I pull it out of my pocket and walk out of the bathroom. When I see Victor's name on the screen, I debate ignoring his call. He knows I was going to dinner with our potential clients tonight, and I'm sure that he wants to know if I've gotten any closer to sealing the deal.

Further away actually.

Sighing, I slide my thumb across the screen and press the Speaker icon.

"Hey, Victor," I say as friendly as I can, not wanting him to fire me if he suspects I've been drinking with the clients. I mean, drinking isn't prohibited, but drinking so many glasses of wine that you decide you kind of want to bone one of the men you're supposed to be convincing to sell? Yeah . . . that's too far.

"Hey, big gun," he says charmingly. "How'd dinner go? Is the ink still wet or what?"

I cringe, chewing my bottom lip as I try to come up with something to say back—and fast. I know what he'll do if I don't seal this deal. *This seemingly impossible deal.* He'll refrain from letting me in on another big opportunity, and he'll send one of his pompous friends next time, even though they won't be able to do it either.

Taking a deep, silent breath, I let it out and roll my shoulders back. I'll be damned if I lead on to him that I'm in over my head. I need to sell it that I'm confident in being here.

"It went well," I say because, frankly, I had a nice time, and the food was to die for. "Though I'll be up front with you; this family isn't going to be an easy nut to crack. They are very stubborn when it comes to this land."

"I'd be a little concerned if they weren't." He barks out an obnoxious laugh. "Find your in and then go from there."

"My in . . ." I murmur, even though I know what he means.

"Yeah, your in," he chimes. "The weakest link. The brick that'll be the first to fall."

"Yeah, no … I knew what you meant," I say softly, pinching the bridge of my nose because I know exactly who the weakest link is.

"Well, I gotta run," he tosses back. "Get a good night's rest because, tomorrow, you need to be back at it." He pauses. "Why don't you take them some baked goods?"

"I don't bake," I say sharply. "At all."

"So, go to the bakery." He pauses. "Gotta go."

He ends the call, and the words replay in my mind over and over again.

"The weakest link. The brick that'll be the first to fall."

It's Tucker. The guy who blushed whenever I looked his way. Some might think it was Riley, but they'd be wrong. Riley is a playboy. He's a good time, and I'd be willing to bet he's damn good in the sack too. But he'd be using me as much as I'd be using him, and that's not the way to get what I want. Sweet, innocent Tucker … he's the one. And yet something about admitting that to myself makes me feel awful.

So, to take my mind off sweet Tucker and the fact that I am considering flirting with the poor man to get what I need, I take my phone out and search for bakeries. Because if I'm going to win any of the Adams family over, it's certainly not going to be with my own baked goods.

Chapter 8

Ridge

I PUT THE LAST PIECE OF BLOCKING UNDER MY OLD MAN'S BOAT TO keep it secured while it sits on land and stand up. What was supposed to be a day out to haul ended up being too rough to get out, so I offered to help him haul his boat out for the winter. While my brothers and I stay out mostly year-round, he stopped winter fishing a while back, and I'm thankful for that because I wouldn't want to worry about him out there on the really rough days. It's not even like he's too old for it, but his boat isn't as big as ours is, and it doesn't have an enclosed wheelhouse to keep him out of the wind.

He calls me and my brothers pussies for having heated wheelhouses and nice, plush captain's chairs to sit in when we sail in after a long day. But deep down, the fucker is jealous but is too damn proud to copy us.

My mom snaps a picture of it on land—just like she does every single year when it goes in and every single year when it comes out. She's bundled up in her coat, hat, and mittens, and unfortunately, when she starts toward me, I know she's got a bone to pick, just by the way she walks like she's on a mission. I have three brothers, so between all four of us, someone is always in trouble. Typically though, it's not even my fault.

"Ridge," she calls out.

My dad gives me a look that tells me, *Good luck.*

"Yeah?"

"I stopped at your house earlier to let Marlin out to pee, and I noticed you don't have a Christmas tree up." She sighs. "You know how I feel about that. I like my boys to at least have a tree in their damn house, and out of all of you, Riley is the only one I don't have to hunt down."

Damn it, Marlin. My lazy French bulldog that my mother considers her grandchild.

The fucker probably didn't even need to go outside; she just worries too much.

I chose an old-man name for him, and it couldn't have been more fitting.

"That's because Riley is an over-the-top weirdo," I deadpan, earning me a leveled stare.

"You have the day off. Christmas is six days away." She gives me a tiny smile, as if testing the waters. "Jon's is open. They probably still have some beautiful trees left to choose from."

I don't know why I continue to fight it each year when I know that I'll end up putting one up at the last minute. But this way, I at least put it off as long as I can. I don't mind having a tree, and I do like Christmas as much as any single grown-ass man can, but I hate fucking with the tree. It's a pain in my ass.

"So, you want me to put a real one in and then catch my house on fire?" I say, like we don't have this same conversation every single year. "And Marlin's gonna piss on it, you know. He always does."

She almost looks amused because she knows that when it comes to her kids and my dad, she gets her way. She puts up with too much shit from all of us to not.

"It's been fine all the other years you've lived alone, hasn't it?" She lifts a questioning brow. "That's what I thought. So, it'll be fine now." She pats my arm. "Do it for your mama. You were a colicky little asshole when you were a child, and your labor was the longest out of all four of you. So, don't make me ask again, love."

She knows my ass will be in my truck in the next few minutes, headed to Crabby Jon's Tree Farm to get a damn Christmas tree that I don't actually give a shit about.

"Fine," I utter. "I'll go get a damn tree. It'll shed all over my house and make a mess."

My mom knows my house will never be a mess. Riley and Easton? The tree could drop its pine needles all through their house, and they wouldn't care. But they also still ask my mom to do their laundry sometimes, and she's hired housekeepers for them before because they are so damn messy. Tucker and I are the clean ones. Everything has a place.

"That's my boy." She winks but then moves her gaze behind me.

Appearing entertained, she wiggles her brows. "Oh, look at that. It seems we have company."

Shifting my body slightly, I crane my neck to look in the direction my mom is staring, and of course, I find Stella bundled up and walking toward us. Even from here, I can tell she's shivering, and in her hands—her very bare hands that should have gloves or mittens on—she holds a box.

"Be nice," my mother mumbles with a hint of warning in her tone before giving my shoulder a small pat.

"She's not nice," I point out. "She's the opposite of nice."

My mom's elbow nudges into my side. "That may be true, but she's also very smart and obviously pretty." She chuckles. "Your brothers all seemed to notice, too, because, my Lord, those boys couldn't keep their eyes off her the other night. Then again, neither could you."

My eyes stay on the redhead, her hair spilling from her beanie down past her shoulders, as she gets closer to us, but I can't stop the scowl that overtakes my face. "No, I wasn't. And what do you mean, my brothers all noticed? Don't they know she's the enemy?"

Yeah, because that's the only reason why I care if they look at her. It has nothing to do with me thinking she's the most beautiful creature in the world. Or me wanting to do wicked things to her mouthy lips. Not at all.

"Well ..." She snickers. "It's just ... Riley was up her ass the entire night, and poor Tuck turned beet red every time she looked his way." She laughs. "Easton was the only one who didn't seem to care that she was there. He hardly looked at her at all actually. But you, Ridge? Don't even try to stand there and say you weren't watching her all night."

A harsh scowl forms on my face, and I can't wipe it off. I don't know if it's because I'm pissed that my mom is accusing me of being into this bitchy city girl or if it's because my brothers are too. The only reason I should be pissed is hearing that my brothers seem interested when we all need to be ice cold to her so that she leaves.

Me included.

"Hi, guys!" Stella says cheerfully, beaming at us as she tries to play it off like she's this ray of fucking sunshine when I know she's not.

When she got out of my truck the other night, after I led her to believe I wanted to fuck her, she was pissed. Now, she's plastering this whole *I am not angry* act. But I'm not buying it. She's two-faced as fuck.

Both faces are pretty. But either way, she's awful.

"Hi there," my mom greets her warmly. "Did you walk here from the rental? It's awfully cold out today for that." She stops, looking Stella all over. "And you don't even have mittens on! You must be freezing."

"Oh, no, I'm fine." Her lip trembles, and her teeth chatter. Looking down at the box, she holds it up. "I went to that adorable bakery in town, and they just had so many options. I figured I'd get some things for you and your family for being so kind and inviting me to dinner the other night."

"You didn't have to do that," my mom says, slowly taking the box. "That was sweet of you though. This looks great," she says, peeking through the clear plastic top at the arrangement of pastries.

"It's the least I could do, really."

Stella's sickly-sweet tone makes me want to throw the box onto the ground and stomp over it. She can fool a lot of people, I'm sure. But she isn't fooling me. It's in her job description to charm people. But underneath that charm? There's a reason for it. A selfish reason, just so that she can get what she wants.

She's basically in the same bracket as a car salesman. You can't trust them, and I can't trust her.

"I'll go put this in the front seat of my car," Mom says, stepping back. "And I think I have an extra set of mittens in there too. You can use them."

"Oh, I'm fine." Stella stuffs her hands into her pockets. "See? All better now."

My mom doesn't say anything else but instead heads to where her car is parked, and I know damn well when she returns, she'll have a pair of mittens.

As soon as she's out of sight, Stella's eyes narrow to slits. "Wipe that smirk off your face, Outlaw. Don't even think those treats were for you."

"You don't have to be bashful, Fireball," I taunt her. "I see what you're up to. You really wanted to have your way with me the other night. I wouldn't let you, so you brought a box of baked goods in hopes it would sweeten me up and make me change my mind." I shake my head, raising my brows playfully. "Sorry, babe. It's not gonna work."

"You're absolutely infuriating," she growls lowly, pulling her hands from her pockets to fold her arms over her chest.

She looks sort of like Tinker Bell right now, only ... one in the North Pole, and instead of blonde hair, hers is auburn.

A huge-ass smirk is tugging at my lips, but I fight it off, even though it's hard. This woman is a goddamn pest. But, Jesus, she's fun to piss off and even more fun to look at when she's mad.

Before I can say something to make her cheeks redder with fury, my mom returns. And just as I suspected, she's holding a spare pair of fuzzy mittens.

"These are brand-new—never been worn, I promise," she says, pushing them toward Stella. "You can keep them. I have about ten pairs."

"I'm really fine, Mrs. Adams," she says, smiling politely. "I just wanted to bring over the bakery goodies and get a bit of fresh air." She glances from my mother to me, bobbing her head. "Think I'll, uh … get going now. I need to run to the market to get a few things."

As she starts to turn, my mom stops her. "Wait," she calls out, probably louder than she meant to, and when Stella looks at her, my mom cocks her head to the side. "Ridge was just going to town to get a Christmas tree. Why don't you catch a ride with him? It's supposed to snow a bit in the next hour or so; it could get slippery on the roads."

I crane my neck to give my mother a glare, but she keeps her eyes fixed on Stella.

"Oh, uh …" When Stella pauses, I look at her to find her eyes on mine. "That's okay. I'm sure Ridge wants to do that alone—or with someone. Just not … me." She swallows harshly. "I'll get back before the snow starts, I'm sure."

Stella holds her hand up to wave before turning again, but this time, she starts to actually walk away. I know my mom isn't going to let this go, but it's still worth a try.

"Well, guess I'd better get going before all the trees sell out," I utter, turning on my heel. I don't even turn away before my mom's hand is on my arm.

"Hold your horses, boy," she warns. "You're taking her with you. It's the polite thing to do."

I stare at her in disbelief because why in the hell would my mother want any of her sons to hang around a woman like Stella, who is here, acting like our land is a piece of fucking meat at the grocery store? She doesn't get it. To Stella, all her and her colleagues see is dollar signs.

"Mom," I grumble, "she's annoying. I couldn't give two shits about a tree. I'm doing it for you though because for some reason, you hate the thought of me enjoying *not* having to water a goddamn tree or sweep up its damn pine needles. Now, you want me to take *her*?" I jerk my chin up the driveway, where Stella is getting farther and farther away. "She's the enemy."

"And that right there is why I want you to take her," she explains. "If Riley took her, he'd fall in love, and I don't trust her just yet. If Tucker took her, he'd melt the first time she spoke to him, and she'd take our land." She pats my back. "But you, Ridge? I know damn well that she'll never get anywhere with you when it comes to this shorefront. But it's almost Christmas. And instead of being back in the city with her friends and family, preparing for the holidays, she's here, working on something that she'll never win. The least you can do is take the damn girl to the tree farm."

I open my mouth to tell her another reason why I don't want to take this woman with me, but she gives me her signature look. It's the look that says, *Shut the fuck up, boy, and do what you're told. I created your ass.*

"Fine," I gripe.

Soon, I'm groaning and sulking as I make my way toward my truck. Just before I get to it, my dad emerges from the other side of the boat, where he was rechecking the blocking for the tenth time.

"Where are you off to?" he hollers.

"Crabby Jon's," I say, sounding as unimpressed as I actually am.

"Oh fuck," he mumbles. "Have fun with that."

"Yeah. Right," I say before climbing in my truck and slamming the door.

It's one thing to enjoy getting under Stella's skin. It's another to go to a fucking Christmas tree farm with the woman and pretend like I don't absolutely hate her.

Stella

I fight back a shiver when I hear a truck driving closer to me as I head back up the driveway that leads to the lobster pound owned by the Adams. I'm a New Yorker, so cold winters are nothing new to me, but in New York, I'm not trudging through no-man's land with the cold ocean air whipping in my face the way I am right now. My fingers, even now in my pockets, feel like they may fall off. I should have taken those mittens.

From the corner of my eye, I see Ridge's truck rolling beside me and hear his window rolling down. I don't stop walking though, and I don't turn to look at him either.

"Go away, Outlaw," I say, taunting him—because who names their boat *Eastern Outlaw*? I mean, for real.

Even if the name is pretty hot …

"Get in," he calls, sounding much less than impressed.

I tap my chin thoughtfully. "Hmm … let me think about it. Nah, I'll pass," I say, cringing inwardly because I'm sure Victor would kill me if he found out that I rejected a ride from one of the key people I'm supposed to be getting close to for this land. I can't help myself though. I already thought the man was a dick, and after last night, when he played me like a fucking piano … yeah, no way am I getting in the truck with this motherfucker. *Hell no.*

"Look, my mom is watching," he practically growls. "So, if I drive off and leave your ass walking, she'll show up at my house later and tear me a new asshole."

I turn toward him, still keeping my legs moving as I trudge along the paved driveway and laugh. "You mean I get to turn you down *and* make your mom mad at you?" I give him a little smirk. "Consider me sold."

His eyes narrow, and there's absolutely no humor on his face. "I'll throw you over my shoulder and strap you in the front seat of my truck, Fireball," he warns me with a narrowed gaze. "Do not tempt me."

I look forward, knowing that if I can just get around the corner, his parents won't be able to see any of what's about to happen, and so I won't look like a lunatic. I'm not getting in the truck with this man—especially not after he made me feel like a complete fool last night. Over my dead body will I allow myself to look like a fool again. Because that's what Ridge Adams does—he makes me turn into a fucking idiot.

I walk a bit faster and crane my neck to see that the wharf is no longer in sight. When I glance at Ridge, he glares.

"Don't even think about it," he hisses, knowing exactly what I'm about to do.

I'm not going to let this man throw me over my shoulder when I could just walk the whopping half of a mile back to my rental house. Ridge is not the one I need to be focusing on to get this land. In fact, he's the only one I know I will never get anywhere with when it comes to sealing this deal.

So, I do what any sane woman would do when an asshole of a man is driving alongside her—even if he is insanely good-looking.

I run.

I run really freaking fast and hope that if I cut through the woods, it'll connect to the rental's driveway, and I can get inside and lock my door, all before Ridge Adams catches up to me.

"What the fuck?!" he calls behind me.

The faint sound of a truck door opening and slamming shut has me picking up my pace. I don't think he'd chase me, but then again, he just threatened to throw me over his shoulder, so who actually knows?

Seeing a small opening through the woods, I dart off the driveway and head into the trees. I hear his feet crunching right behind mine. My heart races so hard that my chest actually hurts, and my legs suddenly feel shaky from the anticipation. I can't explain this feeling that's filling my body, knowing he could catch me at any given second. It's like fear ...

And excitement.

I've had a lot of clients, but this love-to-hate shit we have going on? This is a first. And hopefully a last, too, because it's extremely inappropriate.

I turn around for a split second to see he's almost caught up to me, but when I look forward again, I see my own driveway is less than ten feet away.

I'm nearly there, just a little further and—

My thought is soon interrupted when my foot catches on a tree root, and my body begins to launch forward.

I brace for impact, though I'm pretty sure the embarrassment is going to hurt much more than my body hitting the ground. But as I'm about to smash into the cold earth, a set of rugged arms wraps around me, pulling me backward to a hard chest, covered in a thick sweatshirt.

Even once I'm back on my feet, Ridge's arms remain around my waist. My chest is heaving, and I don't even know if it's from running, almost falling, or being this close to a man I truly can't stand.

"Jesus Christ, you're fast," he murmurs, huffing out a breath against the back of my head.

I hate the way my skin tingles and how butterflies take flight in my stomach when he's so close. I don't even know this man; all I know is that he listens to his mother, he seems to enjoy being on his boat, *and* he's a douchebag. Other than that, we're strangers, and yet, every single time we're remotely close, my legs turn to limp noodles.

I step forward to pull out of his hold, but instead of releasing me, he spins me to face him and plants his hands on my upper arms.

He gazes down at me, his blue eyes cutting mine like a knife. My brain threatens to go foolish again, but I fight it off, knowing that he's toying with me, just like he did the other night.

"Thank you so, so much for grabbing me like a damn stuffed animal, asshole," I grumble, glaring up at him. "You do realize you're, like, twice my size, right?"

The corner of his lips pulls up the tiniest bit. "I think the correct thing to say would be *thank you*, Fireball. Maybe next time, I'll let you eat shit on the ground instead."

"Please do; it'd be better than being this close to you."

His smirk only grows with every word that comes from my mouth as I attempt to tell him to piss off.

"Is that any way to talk to the man who just saved you?" He tsks me. "Also, that's certainly no way to do business, is it, sweetheart? Being all mouthy like that surely won't get you any closer to getting what you want."

He may like to play with me, but I'm also aware that when he chased me through the woods, his mother wasn't even in sight anymore, yet he did it anyway. So, maybe I have the ability to play with him too. And I'm going to find out.

I stumble a few feet backward, pushing my back against a tree and bringing him right along with me. As I cock my head to the side, my lips curve up. "We both know you're not going to be my client. You're too much of a stubborn asshole for that." I shrug. "Besides, I've never had a client chase me through the woods just to get his hands on me."

"Yeah, well, have to try to keep my mother happy," he mumbles sharply. "I'd rather be doing anything besides this, trust me."

"Your mom couldn't even see us anymore, big guy." I bite down on my bottom lip. "It's obvious that you're just too … obsessed. Business and obsession don't mix, you know."

"What are you talking about?" he snarls, keeping that same

unimpressed expression on his face, though I watch it falter slightly. "Me? Obsessed with you? Pfft. You're not only bitchy; you're fucking insane too."

I'm getting under his skin, and I'm loving every second of it. It's like playing with a favorite toy just before you decide you don't like it anymore and you toss it back into the bin. Ridge Adams might not know that's how I see him, but in this moment, it's exactly like that.

"Well, I mean, it's obvious that you're not the person I should be trying to pursue into selling. It's clear I need to ... *target* someone else." I let a thoughtful expression cover my face. "Someone who is sweet and maybe a little shy. That way, he can hear my ideas."

I'm talking in codes, and yet, right away, it's evident he knows what I'm hinting at, just like I hoped he would.

He leans his head down, hovering his face just above mine. "Stay away from Tucker," he snarls. "I mean it," he says coldly. "Actually, stay away from all of my brothers."

"Or else what, big fella?" I coo. "What exactly are you going to do?"

For a moment, he's silent. Though his breathing is angry and ragged as his stupidly delicious minty breath hits my face. He lifts his hand, gripping my chin.

"For starters, I got a feelin' your boss wouldn't be too impressed with you calling me names." He swallows. "Or you getting drunk at my parents' house and then trying to seduce me."

I make sure to keep myself even, not giving him a single inkling that I'm worked up.

"But the tricky thing is, it'll be your word against mine, big guy," I whisper, keeping my confidence high. "And FYI ... I can be quite convincing."

I lift my hand up, pressing my palm to his abdomen, and even through his thick hoodie, I can feel his body shaking. But I don't think it's with anger. No, this is from breathing heavily because just like I planned, I've gotten him worked up.

"So, don't play with me, *asshole*," I whisper sweetly. "You won't win. That's a promise."

His fingers tighten on my chin, and heat pumps from between my thighs, even though I play it off like I'm bored.

"You know, I could give you what I know you so badly want," he drawls lowly before dipping his lips down to my ear. "And, no, I'm not talking about my family's land, sweetheart. I'm talking about my cock."

A shiver runs down my spine, and my nipples harden under my jacket. I don't say anything as his lips remain close to my ear.

"Hate-fucking can be real fun, you know," he coos. "And we sure have a lot of hate to fuck out, don't we?"

I think my soul leaves my body for a moment and my brain grows completely fuzzy. I have no doubt he knows what he's doing in bed. But I'm not falling for his tricks this time. So, instead of making a fool of myself, I lean my head back and gaze up at him, doing my best to look dazed by his words. And let's be honest ... I don't have to try too hard.

"Hmm ... that sounds ..." I let my palm skim down his abdomen, getting lower and lower to his belt while my eyes float to his lips.

It's him who is looking like a dazed mess. Just as he leans closer and his lips are hovering over mine, I give his chest a shove, sending him stumbling a few feet back from me, and then I bolt.

"That sounds awful, sucker!" I call out, so sure that this time, I've won this battle.

But I should have known better because my five-foot-two body can't run away from him. And seconds later, just like he told me he would, I'm thrown over his shoulder while he turns back toward where his truck is.

"Put me down!" I pound my fists against his back. "This is illegal! I could have you arrested!"

"Oh, yeah?" he deadpans, completely unfazed. "Try it, and I'll just say there's a crazy lady poking around my property, acting like a weirdo." He gives my ass a few light smacks. "Spoiler alert: the police officers are all friends of the family."

I continue to pound his back and add my feet kicking into the mix simply for the hell of it. "Just put me down, will you?"

"Sweetheart, you couldn't fight your way out of a wet paper bag. So, cut the shit."

He continues to walk toward his truck, and I think my fingers may actually be icicles now, and all I want is to be back inside my rental house, eating the doughnuts I bought earlier and watching crime documentaries.

Keeping my body slung over his shoulder like a damn toy, he uses one hand to open the passenger door of his truck before plopping me in the seat. Once I'm in, he reaches around and buckles my seat belt.

"I can buckle myself, you know," I growl up at him. "I'm not a child."

"Could've fooled me," he mutters, hovering just inches above my head with his. "If you sit here like a good girl, I'll take you back to your place. If you try to run again, I'll chase you down, and next time, I'll handcuff you to something."

Why are my thighs attempting to clench together? Good God. I need to get the sudden image of being handcuffed to Ridge's boat while he does dirty things to my body out of my mind. *Seriously. What. Is. Going. On. With. Me?*

I inhale sharply, keeping a firm glare on his face. "Fine," I hiss through gritted teeth, even though inside, my body is tingling, still thinking about the damn handcuffs.

"Good girl," he whispers, making the images in my head get even dirtier.

Thankfully, before I have to wipe the drool from the corner of my mouth, he steps back and closes my door. I consider running again, but what's the use? He'll just keep catching me.

And here I thought, I was a fast runner.

Once he's in the truck, he slams it into drive, and within seconds, we're speeding down the driveway. When we reach the end, he turns left, but instead of pulling down into my rental's driveway, he drives right by it.

"What the hell are you doing?" I bark out, whipping my head around to watch as the sign for my road gets further away. "You said you were going to take me home!"

"Yeah, I had to do that so you'd stop being a crazy person," he drawls. "Your running bullshit took up too much time, and it's going to start snowing soon. So, I'm taking your ass to the store after I get my stupid fucking tree."

Panic arises in my gut when I realize this means I'll have to go to the tree farm too. I hate tree farms. I hate looking at all the families and people who love each other and their stupid, happy faces while they choose a tree that they are going to throw outside weeks later.

"I live in New York, not Florida," I grumble. "I can drive in the snow."

"Driving in the middle of a city when it snows is different from here, where people are driving fifty to sixty miles an hour." He glances over at me, winking. "Besides, you can help pick out a tree. Maybe it'll make you more cheerful."

"I ... no." I shake my head. "I don't want to go to the tree farm. Can you just ... can I—just drop me off at the store, and then go get your tree and you can pick me up after." I pause. "Or I can hitchhike. That sounds more fun."

He's quiet, looking from me and back to the road. "Why don't you want to go get a Christmas tree?" he asks, only this time, his voice holds a certain softness in it. "Are you a tree-hugging hippie who can't stand the sight of all the chopped-down trees?" He narrows his eyes and grins. "Although tree huggers don't typically have diets that consist of Toaster Strudels and crunchy Cheetos. So, I'm going to go ahead and guess that isn't it."

I blush, remembering he saw—and paid for—my whole basket of crap I bought the first night we met and knowing that when we stop at the store on the way home, I need to stock up on Toaster Strudels once again.

"I just don't like Christmas." I shrug, playing it off like it's no big deal because I don't want him to dig further into it. "And places like tree farms just aren't my cup of tea."

There's that look I knew I'd get. It's the same one I get from every single person when they find out I don't love the holiday that everyone else thinks is so damn magical.

"You don't celebrate Christmas?"

"No," I say, probably a little too snappy. I'm not going to tell him that I don't celebrate Thanksgiving either. I don't have time to go over that with him too.

"Is it, like, a religious thing?" he asks, continuing to look back and forth from the road to me.

"Nope," I say bluntly. "It's a me thing."

"Oh, okay." He nods his head subtly, like he doesn't know what to say. He's quiet for a moment before he shrugs. "Look, I don't love the tree farm either. It just means a lot to my mother if I put a stupid tree up in my house. Don't ask me why." When we come to a Stop sign, he looks over at me. "What if we call this hatred we have for each other a truce—just for today—and you come with me anyway?" He gives me the tiniest smile. "I'll be fast, I promise."

I inhale sharply, blowing it out. This is the first time since the banana incident that I've seen Ridge be soft. Maybe I can use this to my advantage to get him to hear me out on Ironbound's proposal. I need to think about my career here, so finally, I shrug.

"Fine. But I still hate you."

"And I can't stand you either," he says, grinning.

And for whatever reason, suddenly . . . I feel something I never feel. I feel freaking bashful. And I hate every second of it.

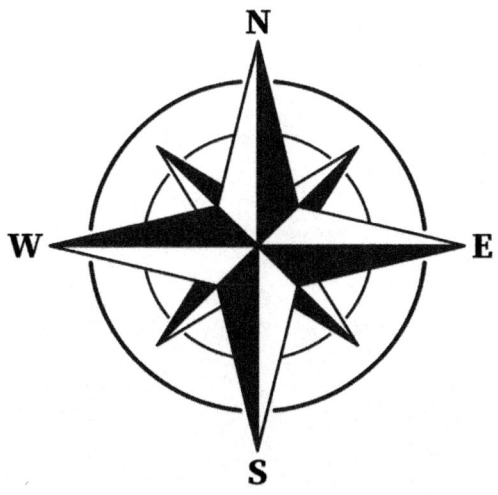

Chapter 9

Ridge

JUST WHEN I THOUGHT I HAD THIS COMPLICATED HUMAN FIGURED out, I bring her to a tree farm, and she's walking around like a lost puppy dog. She typically has a sharp look on her face, but right now, she just looks sad.

And suddenly, I feel like a dick for making her come to this place with me.

It's spitting snow now, and with the freezing temperature, it's fucking cold out. Stella is better dressed than me—aside from the sneakers she's wearing, which are not waterproof.

"What do you think of this one?" I ask, nudging her side gently and pointing to a tree. "It doesn't look too bad."

She eyes it over and shrugs. "They all look the same to me. I'm not sure I'm the best wingman for this."

I rear my head back before I gaze around at the row of trees beside us. "I mean, that one right there is short and stubby. And the one beside it? It looks like another tree tried to fuck it and got too rough and ripped half its limbs off. That guy at the end? That's what I would call a Charlie Brown tree. And the one across from it is overkill and would totally piss my brothers off because my Instagram story on Christmas night would, hands down, kick the shit out of theirs."

"So, pick that one then," she says, completely disconnected from what we're here for.

I don't know what it is, but seeing her like this—so down in the dumps—makes me look at her differently. Since the first time we met, when she got pissed at me for buying her groceries, I've thought she was a coldhearted bitch. Now, I think she's just a sad girl, hiding behind that icy attitude.

"Fine," she says quickly, a fed-up expression on her face before her finger points at the Charlie Brown tree. "That's the one. That's your winner." She claps her hands. "Pack it up. Let's get the fuck out of here."

I know she thinks I'll call her bluff and say obviously that's not the tree I'm getting because it's definitely the ugliest son of a bitch here. But in reality, I don't give a fuck what my tree looks like. Hell, I don't really even want one to begin with because my dog likes to mark his territory on it every year and I have to put a damn baby gate around the fucking thing so that he can't get to it.

Instead of arguing, I look it up and down and bob my head. "Looks good," I say, chipper, and walk over to it.

Soon, she's hastily trailing behind me while I walk around to the back of it.

"Wait, wait. I mean … I was kind of joking." She stops, and I glance over to find a grimace on her face. "Or maybe being a bit bitchy." She pauses. "Yeah. Definitely bitchy." She sighs, brushing her hands against the tree. "Your mom will want you to have a beautiful tree. And despite my distaste for you, I really like your mom. You'd better get a different one."

I doubt she actually likes my mom. But I can see the wheels turning in her head. I'm sure she's thinking that if I get this ugly-ass tree and then I tell my mom it was her idea, my mom will be mad. If my mom's mad, she won't be as kind to her hanging around and still pushing this shit about us selling our land to her company.

Even when she's being sulky and sad, she's thinking about that fucking career.

"My mom doesn't give a fuck what the tree looks like. Just that we all have one," I say truthfully.

I take one look at her, and I can read her like a book and see how uncomfortable she is right now. I might not like her, and she may be in Maine for all the wrong reasons, yet, for some strange reason … I want to cheer her up.

Stepping in front of her, I rest my hands on my waist. "How about this, Miss Difficult as Fuck? We'll go to the store and get the ugliest ornaments we can find, and we'll make this the worst-looking motherfucking tree anyone has ever seen." I grin at her. "You can hate on Christmas and beautiful, picture-perfect trees all you want." I jerk my chin toward the tree.

"But this one? Nah. There's no way. He's already had a rough enough life without you shitting on him. I mean, just look at the poor guy."

Questioning first flashes on her face, but when she realizes I'm serious, she fights back a smile. "He? The tree has a gender?" She narrows her eyes, looking it over. "I don't see a penis anywhere."

"Don't embarrass him more than he already is," I whisper, and this time, she actually giggles. "He's ugly, *and* he has a small dick. It's tragic really." Reaching forward, I bop her nose playfully with my finger. "What do you say, Fireball?" I wiggle my brows at her playfully. "Challenge accepted?"

She looks down for a second, and I swear, it's almost like she reverts back to a child before, finally, she lifts her head back. "Sure. I mean, it's the least we can do for this poor, ugly-ass, tiny-dick tree. Right?"

"Oh, for sure." I nod quickly before grabbing it. "All right, Mr. Tiny-Dick Tree. You're coming with us."

As I drag the tree toward the front to load it into the back of my truck, I glance next to me. And the weirdest thing happens ...

Stella smiles at me.

But what's even more fucked up? My heart swells, and I smile back.

For the first time since her stuck-up ass landed here, I don't want to wring her neck.

It's a fucking Christmas miracle.

Of course, the moment is going well, until the owner's wife, Mary, suddenly appears out of absolutely nowhere. She's known me my entire life, and she's nice enough, but, goddamn, she's always been extremely pushy with just about everything. Especially always wondering why my brothers and I are single. She's made it her personal mission to try to hook each one of us up. This might be my opportunity to never deal with that again.

Her eyes take in the sight of me and Stella, and I cringe.

I lean closer to Stella's ear. "I'm really sorry for whatever is about to happen."

Before she even has the chance to ask what in the hell I'm talking about, Mary has her camera out and is fast approaching us.

"Ridge! I thought that was you over here, next to this gorgeous girl." She beams at both of us, practically bouncing before holding her camera up to me. "You know how we feel about documenting our customers' experiences. So, you two lovebirds need to come sit on the steps in front of the Crabby Jon's sign!"

Stella's eyebrows form a straight line, and she opens her mouth to no doubt argue. "Oh, we're not a co—"

"That sounds great, Mary," I cut her off, smiling at Stella and nodding slowly. "Doesn't it, babe?"

Casting a glare straight at me, she folds her arms over her chest. "Why, yes, Ridge, that sounds absolutely delightful."

The words come out sounding like she's a robot, and I try not to laugh at her enthusiasm, but it's not easy.

I wave my hand toward the steps, knowing this drill because there were times in the past when I had to take a picture all by myself with a damn tree I didn't give a fuck about getting. If you stop in when Mary isn't here, you're in luck because no one else gives a shit about these pictures. But if she's here? Shut the fuck up and take the picture because she'll likely follow you home if not.

I sit down, and right away, she tries to sit a foot away; instead, I tug her down in front of me, pulling her in real close.

"What the hell are you doing, asshole?" she whispers.

"Just sit there and smile like a good girl," I warn her. "Don't you see the crazy in her eyes? You don't want that smoke."

Just then, she looks at Mary, and I can feel her body begin to shake with laughter, though she does her best to contain it to be polite.

"Fine," she whispers. "I'll play along. But only because you're right. She's a nutjob for sure."

I hold her a little closer, feeling her relax against me as Mary snaps a picture.

"Okay, you're all set." She beams at us. "Thank you for your business, lovebirds. Be sure to tag us on Facebook once your tree is up!"

And then, thank fuck, she's off to bug the shit out of someone else.

"Clearly, she didn't see the tree we'd picked out." Stella snorts, but after a few seconds, she realizes that she's still leaning against me and scurries to get up.

Typically, I hate to see Mary coming. But after she just made Stella take a picture and pretend to actually like me?

Well, I may just be her biggest fan.

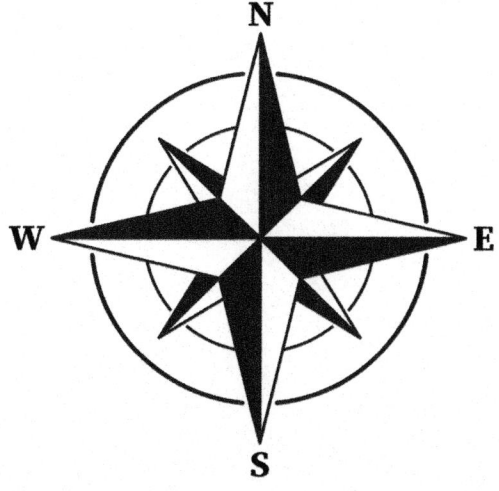

Chapter 10

Stella

RIDGE AND I CONTINUE TO FILL OUR CART WITH UGLY CHRISTMAS decorations. And between choosing a homely tree; grabbing lunch at one of the cutest restaurants I've ever seen, called The Rusty Anchor; and now this … I can't believe I'm going to admit it, but … I've actually been enjoying myself today. I'm certainly not going to boost Ridge's ego and tell him that because he'd never let me live it down, but it's the truth. And I made it through the tree farm experience without breaking down or kicking the shit out of any innocent trees.

Winning.

"What about these? These are fucking terrible," Ridge says, holding up a box of brown ornaments. "They look like shit with sparkles dumped on them."

I laugh, taking them from him and putting them in the cart. "Yep. We're definitely getting those."

Something about this—about not decorating the perfect tree just to pretend everything is wonderful—well, it somehow makes me not hate doing it. In fact, I'm kind of liking it. And Ridge and I haven't even fought. Not once.

Grabbing a Santa hat from the rack, he leans forward and carefully pulls it down onto my head. But instead of moving away after, he hovers, looking down at me.

"Well," he drawls lowly, "aren't you cute?"

My cheeks heat, and I fight an awkward giggle.

"Keep it. I like how it looks on you, Fireball."

He swallows, staring down at me, and I stand here, still as a statue and completely incapable of moving.

My eyes pause on his lips, and for a moment, there are no other sounds in the grocery store. Or at least, I can't hear them because all I can hear is my heart pounding. But when a loud voice comes through the intercom for a cleanup in aisle eleven, I blink a few times and pull myself together.

Reaching for the top of my head, I tug the hat off, but when I go to step around him to hang it back up, he grabs it from my hand.

"Oh no, you don't, Fireball." He tsks me. "If we're going to make my tree ugly as hell, you've got to wear this while we do it." He tosses it into the cart.

I roll my eyes, but then suddenly, I smirk at him. "Well then, fine, so do you," I taunt him before grabbing a second one. "If I have to wear an ugly-ass red hat, so do you."

I expect him to change his mind and say hell no. After all, he certainly doesn't seem like the type of man who is going to wear a damn Santa hat while decorating a tree with someone who is practically a stranger. But he doesn't fight it. Instead, he shrugs.

"Well, okay then." He looks away from me and toward the cart. "That should do it, yeah?" he says, narrowing his eyes. "That creepy lobster on top is really going to be the finishing touch, huh?"

"Uh … duh." I nod quickly, looking at the lobster with the huge eyes that seem to watch me wherever I go. "That thing may haunt me in my nightmares."

As we start toward the register, with Ridge pushing the cart beside me, I chew my lip nervously. "Hey, I just have to go grab some socks. I'll meet you up front?"

"Uh, yeah, sure." He stops the cart, looking down at my feet. "Your sneakers got wet at the tree farm, didn't they?"

"It's no big deal; they'll dry," I assure him, even though I don't know why he'd care. "Just gonna grab some socks to get me through the ride home."

"Come on," he murmurs, nodding his head for me to follow him.

I trail behind him as he leads us into the part of the store that has shoes. But he doesn't just stop and tell me to look around. No, he's on a mission for something specific. And rather than fight it or ask questions, like I do ninety percent of my life, I just let him lead the way.

"You need some of these. The ground's wet. You're always walking around with that damn iPad, falling more in love with land you'll never get to have." He smirks, winking. "These boots are where it's at, I'm telling you." He points down to his own feet, showing me that he has a pair of black ones on. "I can promise you, my feet aren't wet."

I gaze at the display of short rubber boots before I read the tag. "Xtratuf?" I read the name out loud. "Aren't these for, like … fishing?"

"Nah, we all wear the tall ones when we go to haul," he says, picking up a pair of the boots and looking them over. "These ones are called deck boots, but they are for day-to-day shit. And super comfortable and waterproof." He sets those down before grabbing another. "These ones are insulated, which would be better for you since it's going to be cold all week."

I frown, scrunching my nose up. "They aren't that cute, you know."

"Neither were those high-heeled boots you had on the first day we met," he retorts, continuing to look through the display. "Yet you put those on."

He even knows what kind of shoes I had on the first day he saw me.

Taking out a pair of gray ones, I spin them around to look at them. On the backs is a subtle design with blue lobsters. They aren't the prettiest boots I've seen—that's for sure. But they are also not the ugliest. In fact, every second that passes, they seem to be growing on me.

Grabbing a pair of women's eights, I sit down on the bench and slide off my wet sneakers when suddenly, Ridge is grabbing a pack of socks and ripping them open to hand me a pair.

Looking from him to the socks, I rear my head back. "Look, you may refer to yourself as Outlaw, but I'm not about breaking the law." I point to the socks. "And I'm certainly not stealing socks."

He gives me a judgy look. "I'm going to pay for them up front when I pay for your boots, crazy." He thrusts the socks into my hands. "Throw your other ones away. They probably smell like ass anyway."

Reluctantly, I pull off my soaked socks, tossing them into the small trash bin before yanking on the new ones and then the boots. Standing up, I take a few steps, looking down at my feet. "Okay, I'll admit … they are comfortable."

When my eyes move back to him, I'm met with a grin. "Told ya."

Grabbing my sneakers, he puts them into the now-empty box before setting it in the cart. "Now you won't have to wear those wet sneakers home," he says like a true smart-ass, but when I stare at him, surprised, he shrugs. "Since, you know, they probably smell too. Come on. It's time to go put our tree up."

I'm still absolutely shocked by how sweet this man is being to me. And when we walk toward the register, I'm taken aback even more when he says, "You get in line, and I'll go grab you some of those disgusting Toaster Strudels." He pauses. "Strawberry, right?"

For a moment, all I can do is stare because just a few hours ago, he was being an asshole.

But after a second, I nod. "Y-yeah. That's the one."

Maybe he's playing me. Or perhaps he's doing whatever he can to keep me away from his brothers. I don't really know why he's being so kind and thoughtful today. All I know is ... I can't let it cloud my judgment. The reason why I'm here hasn't changed, even if his temperament has.

Once the last ornament is hung, Ridge plops down on the couch with his dog, Marlin, before admiring our terrible job.

Ridge tugs the Santa hat from his head as he looks at the tree, pleased with what we just did. Me? I stand back and look at our masterpiece, grimacing.

"This is so terrible that I almost feel bad for you," I say, somewhere between laughing and cringing. My hat came off about ten minutes ago because my head was damn near sweating. Ridge gave me shit when I peeled it off, but I couldn't help it. "You have this extremely dreadful tree in this beautiful house. It just feels so wrong."

Ridge's house is gorgeous. It's all cathedral ceilings and huge windows. It's modern with a hint of rustic farmhouse. And it's immaculate. Which, I learned when we first got here, is because he's a neat freak, and I can appreciate that because I'm the same way.

It's not what I imagined his bachelor pad might look like, and I really do feel like we did his home dirty by bringing this tree and its ugly-ass ornaments here.

"I think it looks good." He gives Marlin a few pats on his stomach, and the dog literally does nothing.

In the hour or so I've been here, he's snored, farted, and slept.

"If Mama Adams stops over, this was your idea," I warn him. "Don't be throwing me under the bus, big guy."

"She won't be over tonight. It's snowing, and when it's snowing, my parents make popcorn and watch movies." He tells me this like it's absolutely no big deal. As if his parents aren't doing shit that is in romance novels and rom-coms or something, even though they've got to be in their fifties.

When he catches me gawking at him, he shrugs. "What?"

"They make popcorn and watch movies?" I gasp. "Together? Like . . . the two of them?"

"Yeah?" He looks at me like I'm a nut. "They've been married for thirty years. They do weird, boring shit, okay? But it makes them happy."

"That's the cutest thing I've ever heard," I squeak. "Who chooses the movie?"

"My mom," he says instantly. "Always."

"What if she chooses a cheesy rom-com?"

"Then they watch a cheesy rom-com." He relaxes back. "You saw my parents, right? My mom says jump, and my dad says how high, all while he has a smile on his face. That's their dynamic."

I'm twenty-eight years old. I've dated plenty of men, and I've had three semi-serious boyfriends, yet not one of them ever did that for me. I thought I was the problem, or maybe men just all sucked. Maybe I'm wrong.

"That's . . . really cool," I whisper, taking a seat on the other end of the couch. "You're really lucky that your family is so . . . well, strong."

Right when those words leave my lips, I know that I've set myself up for questions about my own family. So, before Ridge gets a chance to blurt anything out, I peek at my watch.

"I should probably get going." I glance at Marlin and then Ridge, daring to look him in the eye. "Today, surprisingly, . . . didn't suck. So, at the risk of you teasing me later for saying this, thank you. For getting me out of my own head."

"Didn't suck, huh?" He grins. "Is that your way of saying you had a good time, Fireball?"

Rolling my eyes, I bite my lip to hold in a laugh. "I mean, I suppose it wasn't *too* bad."

As I stand up, he stands too.

"You know, tomorrow, we go back to hating each other. There's still about six hours left of our truce. Why don't you stay for dinner?" He cringes. "I don't have anything fancy, but I definitely have some boxes of Kraft mac and cheese and probably some tater tots."

"I may be from the city, but when it comes to food, I'm pretty basic." I laugh. "I mean, I live off Toaster Strudels, crunchy Cheetos, and Coca-Cola." I smile. "You had me at the word *Kraft*. And tater tots?" I nod. "Consider me sold, big guy."

"That reminds me; don't forget those when I take you home," he says. "But if you do, trust me, they'll be here when you remember them. Toaster Strudels are gross."

My mouth hangs open. "I am going to pretend you didn't say that. After all, we're having a good evening."

I know I should be going. Nothing good can come out of prolonging hanging out with Ridge, and it'll only complicate the business side of things even more. But today was fun. And I'm not quite ready for that to end.

Besides, what am I going to do at home? Watch a crime documentary?

"All right then, let's go cook a terrible dinner to go along with our ug-ly-ass tree." He grabs my hand and leads me into the kitchen.

Toying with the asshole side of Ridge Adams when we hate each other is fun and a little sexy. But spending the day with the sweet side of him … that might be even better.

Ridge

I think, tonight, I've laughed harder than I've probably ever laughed before. As much shit as I give Stella, she gives it right back to me. She covers her mouth and throws her head back, and tears spring into her eyes. Her auburn hair swings around when she shakes her head and tries to gain composure.

I keep asking myself the same question over and over again. *How the hell am I going to go back to hating her tomorrow?*

Once our laughter subsides, she steps down from the barstool and takes our plates around to the other side of the island before setting them in the sink.

"You don't have to clean up," I say, standing.

"You bought me socks and boots—even though I told you not to," she says, giving me the same look she did in the store when I paid for them before she could get her card out. "And then you cooked dinner. Please, let me clean up. Otherwise, I'm going to be insatiable, and I'll make you call me princess while you bring me food and rub my feet."

"I mean, I'm not really a feet guy but—" I tease her, but when I get around to where she's standing, she slaps my arm lightly.

"Seriously," she utters, looking up at me but suddenly seeming nervous of my presence. "Before you take me back to my place, let me clean up. Besides, before the clock strikes twelve and I hate your guts again, better take advantage of this offer."

She may be talking about her offer to clean up dinner, but all I can think about is taking advantage of the fact that she doesn't hate me right now and how much I'd love to have her in my bed. Then again, I think it would have been fun to bury my cock inside her when she did hate me.

Before I have time to answer, she's in front of the sink, rinsing the plates before putting them into the dishwasher. As she moves to wipe down the countertop, I know I shouldn't get too close, but instead of sitting my ass back down, I walk behind her, grab the bottle of cleaner, and reach around her side to spray some onto the granite countertop, brushing my body slightly against hers when I do.

I'm so close to her that my nose almost grazes her neck when I lean forward. A slight exhale escapes her lips, and when she bends closer to the counter to wipe it, her ass pokes out, barely grazing my jeans, and my cock twitches in reaction. I'm not sure if she felt it or not, and even though I know damn well I need to take her back to her place before something happens between us that we can't take back, I can't seem to back away.

I have to have her—at least once. If not, I'll never stop thinking about it.

"Hey, Fireball?" I rasp from behind her, putting one hand on her waist.

She's practically a stranger, so I'm going to shamelessly shoot my shot here because if she tells me to fuck off, what will in matter once she goes back to the city?

"Yeah?" she breathes out, standing up straighter, but not turning around to face me. She doesn't need to though because I can feel her tensing in anticipation, telling me that whatever I'm thinking, she's probably thinking it too.

I don't know if I've lost my mind or if I just can't resist her any longer, but whatever it is has me reaching around her to grip her chin and force her to look back at me. My heart is racing from my being this close to her, making my breathing grow shallow.

"I know we still can't stand each other and all. And tomorrow, we'll hate each other's guts once again because you'll go back to trying to get my land, and I'll go back to not being able to stand your presence." I slide my hand up her body, forcing her to crane her neck to look at me. "But tonight ... maybe we could do something that we won't do again once we're back to normal."

She drags in a shaky breath, her lips parting subtly—proving how turned on she is and making my dick grow even harder against her ass. And I know she feels it now because she wiggles ever so slightly.

"Something we ... *definitely* won't do again," she whispers, swallowing. "Right?"

Sliding my palm against her cheek, I nod. "Yeah. Just this one time."

She leans closer as she drags in a breath. "I mean ... I guess it wouldn't hurt anything if it was just this once, right? Especially since there's no risk of us wanting to do it again."

My cock is steel in my jeans as I press it gently into her ass. Abruptly, I drop my hands to her waist and spin her to face me. Her ass sits against the countertop, and I slide one hand into her hair before I bring my mouth to hers. I could take it slow, but seeing as we only have a few hours left before she's back to being my enemy, I don't have time for that shit.

Besides, something tells me she doesn't want me to go slow.

All I need is one time, and then she'll be out of my system. I can stop fucking my hand in the shower, thinking it's her mouth. And I can also quit imagining handcuffing her and whipping her ass just before I drive my tongue inside of it for her being so damn mouthy. Yes, one time, and all that shit will go away, just like it always has with any other chick I've fucked.

For days, I've wondered what her lips would taste like, and our kiss confirms that, just like I thought, she's sweet. I guess that makes sense because, inside, she's not nearly as sour as she's convinced me she is. But none of that is going to matter tomorrow.

She kisses me back, moaning into my mouth faintly, giving me the green light to go further.

"Fuuuck, my dick is so fucking hard," I growl against her lips before I lift her onto the counter and spread her legs. When I stand between them, I thrust my cock against her leggings. "Feel that, sweetheart?"

"Yes," she groans out frantically before kissing me again. Her palm slides down my abdomen, rubbing the fabric of my jeans, right over my aching cock. "Fuck ... I need this."

"You need what, Stella?" I utter roughly, trying to fight off the fucking whimper that wants to come from my lips when she continues to rub her hand over the bulge in my jeans. "Tell me what it is you need so that I can give it to you." I bury my face against her neck, biting down on her flesh. "Need to hear you say it, sweetheart."

"I need ..." rushes from her lips desperately as I pull back and look at her again. "I need you to fuck me." She says the words so confidently as her hazel eyes bore into mine. "Fuck me like you'll never get to again. Because you won't."

"Right," I rasp. "Because it's just this one time."

"Just this one time," she whispers. "And you'd better make it worth it, Outlaw."

Fuck. She's so fucking bossy. And it only makes my dick that much harder.

Dominant women have never been my type, but I guess for tonight ... they are.

I reach for her shirt, tugging it over her head and leaving her in her bra, making me inhale sharply at her beauty. Bringing my hand down her body, I push on her stomach, silently telling her to lie on her back, and slowly, she does.

Hooking my fingers into the waistband of her leggings, I pull them down, and my heart fucking squeezes because she doesn't have any panties on.

"No panties, sweetheart?" I breathe out. "Fuck ... what a naughty girl you are."

I drop her leggings onto the floor and stare at her sprawled out on my countertop, a glazed look in her eye, and as hot as she is, I need to see her full tits on display. So, I reach down and unclasp it in the front and push it off her shoulders. The air hits her tits, and her pretty pink nipples harden, making me grind my teeth and reach forward to cup them both at the same time. They more than fill my hands up, spilling out and making my mind spin.

"Fuck, these tits are so big and perfect. I can't wait to stick my dick between them."

Taking a step back, I tug my own shirt over my head and unbutton my jeans. Pushing them down over my hips, I shove my briefs down to release my aching cock.

"Lift those legs, baby. And spread them wide," I mutter, palming my dick when she does as she was told. "Jesus Christ," I hiss. "Such a beautiful fucking pussy."

I reach my hand to her face and hold my palm in front of her. "Get my hand nice and wet, darlin'."

She sticks her tongue out and licks my hand before spitting on it, and my dick jumps.

"Fuck, you're so hot," I groan and fist my cock with my soaked hand. "Tell me, Stella, have you ever played with your pussy, thinking about me?"

It may seem like an off-the-wall question, but I've thought about her numerous times when I fucked my hand. So, with any luck, maybe she's done the same.

Her head cranes forward, and her eyes drink in the sight of me jerking myself. "Yes," she confirms as her brows pull together in agony. "Once, when you were on your boat, I watched you."

"Fuuuck," I growl because I didn't think she'd actually tell me the truth. "What did you do? Did you fuck yourself with a toy, or did you use your fingers?"

Her cheeks redden. "I ... went into my room, and I slid my fingers inside of myself."

"Yeah?" I slow my hand on my cock because the thought of her watching me and fucking herself has me almost blowing my load right now. "Did you imagine it was my cock?"

"Yes," she cries out, nodding slowly.

Dipping my head down, I keep my eyes fixated on hers before I spit onto her pussy.

"Show me," I plead. "Now that you're nice and drenched with my spit, show me how you made that pussy come. Fuck yourself for me. Let me stroke my cock while I enjoy the show."

She rakes in a breath so fast that her throat makes a croaking sound. Trailing her hand down her stomach, she brings it between her legs, doing exactly what she was told with zero hesitation.

"That's it, baby," I huff out, my head fucking buzzing. "Show me how you like it."

She takes two fingers and circles them over her clit, lifting her hips slightly in pure need before she slips the same two fingers inside of her heat. As she works them in and out, every so often going back to rubbing her clit, I swallow back a scream because, goddamn, she's so fucking sexy this way.

"Yes," she breathes out, her eyes lost in need. "Fuck … Ridge. Your cock feels so good."

Her talking to me while she's fucking her fingers is enough to make me come, and I keep my hand still, wrapped around the base of my cock, as I will myself not to come so soon.

Her eyes lock with mine, and she rubs the pads of her fingers against her pussy before she lifts her fingers to my mouth.

"Open." She gives me the command sharply.

When I do as told, she shoves her fingers inside of me while using her other hand to sink her fingers back inside her heat. "Good boy. Now taste me, Outlaw. Lick my fingers clean."

Those words and her fingers in my mouth, and I'm fucking gone.

My balls draw up, and even though I don't want to come so fast, I have no control over it. Soon, my dick explodes, and cum erupts all over my stomach, her legs, and the countertop. As soon as the wetness hits her skin and she realizes that little stunt made me come without her even touching me, her back is off the countertop, and she's screaming out while her hips buck against her hand.

With our eyes locked, we both ride out our orgasms, and the second we're done, I quickly wipe my mess up and yank her upward and make it so that she's straddling my waist before I walk us toward the bedroom.

But not before I grab her Santa hat because, if I'm being honest, she looks damn fucking sexy in it, and I need to fuck her while she has it on. After all, it's all I've thought about since we were at the store.

Stella

After Ridge sets me on his bed and finishes undressing, he grabs the red hat and pulls it onto my head. His cock stands tall in front of me, and I suck in a breath of desperation as I fight the urge not to lean forward and taste it.

"You look too hot with this on, Fireball." He runs his finger over the fabric. "But I need to know, have you been a good girl or a bad girl this year?"

Although I'm a Christmas hater, I suddenly don't hate the sexy holiday festivities right now, and I shift around, ready to find out what exactly this man is going to do to me.

"That depends, Outlaw. What do I get if I say I've been a really good girl?" I coo, biting my lip.

His cock visibly jumps, and I fight a whimper before it gets the chance to slip from my lips.

"If you've been a good girl, I'll let you have my dick any way you want it." He runs his thumb over my lips.

"And if I've been bad?" croaks from my throat. "Then what will I get?"

He smirks, his blue eyes a few shades darker now as he stares down at me. "If you've been a naughty girl, that means I get to take you any way I want. As many times as I want." His hand trails down to my neck, and he applies a little pressure. "So, tell me, beautiful, have you been good … or bad?"

"Bad," I say through gritted teeth, slamming my legs together to relieve some pressure. "Really. *Really.* Bad."

His thumb works back to my chin, and he swallows hard. "Well then, I guess I'd better punish you, huh?"

Staring up at him, I nod slowly. "Yes."

"Lie on your back, Stella," he commands. "Because your body is mine right now. And the first thing I'm going to do is fuck those beautiful, big tits."

I'm relaxing back before he even finishes his sentence, making sure to keep my hat on because, for whatever reason, it makes this even hotter than it already is.

Crawling over me, he positions his face to my chest, dragging his tongue between my breasts before moving to each one and running his tongue around my nipple. When he sucks it into his mouth, a moan rushes from my lips, and he smirks before his lips move between them once more.

He spits down on my flesh, soaking my skin.

"Now your tits are ready for me to slide back and forth."

He moves his legs upward, climbing further up my body so that his cock pokes against my chest. When he sinks lower, his length rests against my skin, and his eyes cut to mine.

"Push your tits together, baby. Make them squeeze around my fat cock."

Bringing my hands to the sides of my breasts, I push them together until they are hugging his dick.

"Fuck, my cock is one lucky motherfucker right now," he grits out. "All wrapped up in those perfect tits." He brings his hand to his mouth and bites down on his knuckle. "You're so fucking pretty this way. Ready and desperate to take my cock anyplace I want to put it."

Dropping his hand down, he brings it to my face. "Open wide."

When my mouth opens, he pushes his thumb between my lips while the rest of his hand stretches as he grips the side of my face.

Without any instruction, I begin to suck on his finger as his hips thrust back and forth while he fucks my chest.

"I could blow my load straight to your neck, baby." He drags in a sharp inhale, thrusting faster and making my tits bounce between my hands. "But I'm not sure you deserve the gift of a pearl necklace just yet, naughty girl."

Removing his hand from my face, he reaches behind him and slides his fingers against my heat. "Fuck, you are soaked, aren't you, Fireball?" he croaks, running the pad of his thumb against my clit. "You've been naughty though. I don't know if you've earned my fingers, either."

I whimper, lifting my hips in anguish and pushing my heat against his fingers. They are so close, and yet I need them to slide inside of me.

"I don't think so, baby girl," he taunts me, slowing his movements but keeping his swollen cock between my breasts. "Bad girls don't get to be finger-fucked. You need to earn them."

"Ridge," I whine, "please."

When he doesn't do what I need, I drop one hand and reach around him to slide it between my legs, shoving his hand out of the way. But before

I can push them deep inside my heat, he grabs my wrist, forcing my hand back to my tits.

"Nuh-uh," he coos, his movements stilling completely. "You chose this, baby. I said naughty or nice, and you chose naughty. So, you don't get to come. At least not just yet."

"Ridge." His name rips from my lips, somewhere between a roar and a whine.

But instead of giving me what I want, he simply smirks again.

"You're being so mouthy for a girl on the naughty list." He tsks me. "I think I should fill that mouth with something; that way, you stop whining."

Even through my agony, the throbbing between my legs only intensifies when he moves higher up my body before his cock is nudging my face.

"Open up, Fireball. I'm about to show you what I do to whiny, desperate, naughty girls like you."

My lips fall apart as I inhale a sharp breath because my mind is spinning, but Ridge takes the opportunity to thrust his dick deep into my mouth.

He tastes so good, just like I knew he would, but that doesn't help the throb that's so deep inside of me; everything hurts because I need relief.

"That's it," he groans. "Be a good girl. Suck my dick really good, and maybe, just maybe, I'll put you on the nice list and let you come on my fingers. Or maybe my tongue."

I don't just want to come; I *need* to. But I also need to suck his dick because, right now, it's all I can think about.

Lifting my head slightly, I take him as deep as I can and then push my face even further against his body. When the tip of his cock hits the back of my throat, I gag. But before I can pull back, his fingers grip the hat on my head as he holds me there, only to make me gag again. Finally, he releases me, and after catching my breath for a second, I resume sliding my lips up and down his rigid dick, letting my spit soak every inch of him that I can.

"That's it," he practically grunts. "Take it. Take all of it."

My hand slides down my body, and I move it between my legs again. Pushing two fingers inside of myself, I cry out with his dick in my mouth at the instant relief. But within seconds, he's pulling my hand away.

"You're never going to get off the naughty list if you keep it up," he says, squeezing my hand in his.

With one thrust, his cock is so far down my throat that I feel like I'm choking. And yet, with tears in my eyes, I still need more.

He grips my throat as his balls rest against my face. "I'm getting close, baby. Tell me, are you going to be a good girl and swallow me down?" he asks.

Instantly, I nod.

"Good girl." He barely hisses the words. "I promise that if you take every drop I give you, I'll reward you."

I don't need to do any work because he thrusts in and out of my mouth fast and hard. The only thing I focus on is keeping my lips snug around his hard cock, and within seconds, his movements are more sporadic, and a loud hiss shoots from his mouth. He grips my neck tighter, tilting his chin toward the ceiling.

"Remember …" he grunts, his body practically quivering just as the first bit of saltiness hits my throat. "Every fucking drop."

I take it all, swallowing him eagerly. He keeps his hold on my throat, and his head shifts up, but the moment he's completely finished, his blue eyes gaze into mine as he tries to catch his breath.

Pulling his dick from my mouth, he runs his thumb against my lips.

"Good girl, baby. Now, you can consider yourself on the nice list."

Releasing his hold on my throat, he leans down, capturing my mouth with his and giving me a hard, rough kiss before moving down my body, dragging his tongue along my flesh.

Stopping once his face is between my thighs, he hooks his arms around my legs and forces them to spread wide, pushing my knees up. The second his tongue hits my clit, my fingers grip his hair roughly.

"God … yes," I moan, pulling on his hair as his tongue slides deeper inside of me.

Pulling back, he spits inside of me before diving back in. I squeeze my eyes shut because it feels too fucking good and my brain is fuzzy.

"Look at me while I eat," he growls against my heat, sending my eyes flying open and my neck craning forward.

With his arms, he rocks my pussy harder against his face in a rhythm, making me shudder against the mattress.

Everything inside of me begins to tingle, and I have to fight to keep my eyes open when a warm wave of pleasure crashes over me, thawing my entire being as a loud moan rips from my throat.

I pull his hair tightly as my orgasm hits me like a thousand rocks at one time, and now, I'm not just moaning; I'm screaming.

My vision becomes blurry, and against his command, I squeeze my eyes shut as my pussy continues convulsing against his tongue.

And when I'm finally finished, I have to pry my eyes open because I've never been this relaxed in my life. I feel as light as a feather yet somehow too heavy to try to get up.

So, when Ridge climbs next to me without saying a word and wraps me up in his arms, I don't fight it. Instead, I succumb to my fatigue, and soon … I doze off.

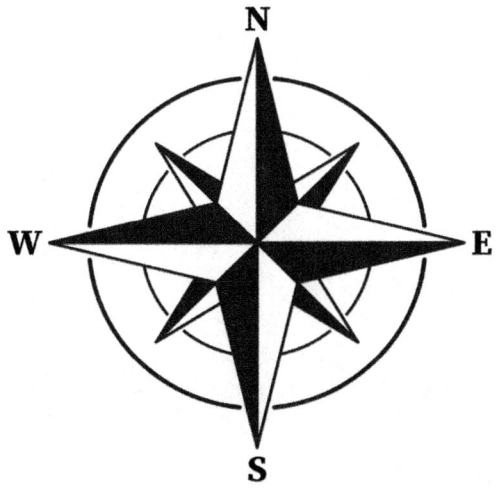

Chapter 11

Stella

W OW. I'M SO COZY, AND THIS IS SO NICE. THIS BED IS SO comfortable. *Why didn't I notice it before?*

My eyes stay closed as I snuggle into the covers, feeling like I could quite possibly fall back asleep. Perhaps it's because this is the best night's sleep I've gotten since being here. After all, how quiet this house is has taken some getting used to. Or maybe I was just really tired after getting some fresh winter air yesterday. Whatever it was made me sleep so soundly, but it's also making me not want to get out of bed. Then again, what do I even have to get up for? I don't even know where to go next to try to convince the Adams that selling out is in their best interest. And I know that soon, Victor is going to wonder what the hell I'm doing here if I'm not making any big moves.

Inhaling and then letting it out in a yawn, I slowly begin to pry my lids open. The room is blurry, and I rub my eyes until finally, my vision clears, and I realize two things. Two not-great things.

One, I'm not even at my rental house. Two, I'm at Ridge's. In his bed.

Oh, and looking down, I realize a third and probably the worst. I'm naked. Completely and utterly naked.

Flipping over, I find the spot beside me empty, but the sound of someone stirring downstairs hits my ears, and I quickly scurry off the bed in an attempt to find my clothes. Every single part of last night rushes through my mind at once, and I relive flashes of all the ways Ridge Adams owned my body.

Although … I feel like I owned his a little too. Especially when I was riding him so hard that his headboard was smashing into the wall and I worried it would break, but I also wasn't concerned enough to stop.

"Shit," I mutter, knowing damn well I never brought my clothes upstairs and that they are likely still scattered throughout the kitchen.

Looking at the bed, I grab the throw blanket that's practically falling off the end and wrap it around myself. My legs feel wobbly, and between my thighs has a dull soreness, only reminding me how far we took the whole *just one night* thing.

Sluggishly, I trudge down the stairs, keeping the blanket wrapped around my body as if the man I'm about to run into hasn't seen what's underneath it.

A vision of Ridge stroking his cock while he watched me pleasure myself assaults my mind. And I almost fall down when I remember how he stopped jerking himself and came all over me, himself, and the counter. All from watching me with my hand between my thighs.

We're supposed to go back to hating each other today, and yet my heart is racing as I think about all the things we did.

I need to get it together.

When I reach the corner that rounds to the kitchen, I hear someone moving around in there. I stop and lean against the wall. Squeezing my eyes shut, I inhale deeply and try to prepare myself to go in, grab my clothing, and act like the professional Victor sent me here to be.

"You gonna stand out there like a weirdo all morning, Fireball?" Ridge's deep voice drawls, sending my eyes flying open. "I can see your shadow. And I heard your footsteps on the stairs."

Grimacing, I stand up taller and push my shoulders back. His back is to me now as he stands in front of the stove, and quickly, my eyes dart around the room to locate my clothing.

"Sorry. I … just," I stutter, "was hoping to find my clothes before … well …"

When he turns around, his blue eyes dance with amusement. "What, before I could see you?" He winks. "All good, Fireball. I've seen what's under the blanket. No need to be bashful. In fact, if you wanted to eat breakfast naked, I wouldn't complain. Actually, if you wanted to stay naked and let me eat my breakfast off of you, I'd even be nice to you for the rest of your days in Maine."

I fight back a squirm as I imagine his head buried between my thighs while I'm sprawled out on the kitchen table. Luckily, the sound of Marlin's toenails snaps me out of it, and he stands beside me, wiggling around for attention.

Leaning down, I scratch his back. "Good morning, Marlin," I coo, giggling when he makes a snorting sound. Slowly, I stand up again and hold the blanket a little tighter. "That sounds fun and all, but I should probably be getting dressed." I chew the inside of my cheek, looking around. "Did you move my clothes?"

Yep. This is probably where our truce ends. He probably burned my clothes, and now he's going to make me ride home naked as punishment.

"You're no fun," he utters, but luckily, he jerks his chin upward toward the table. "I folded them and set them in a pile on the chair at the end."

After a few awkward seconds, I dart toward the table and grab my stuff.

"I'm going to go change," I murmur, chewing the inside of my cheek.

Last night, everything was exciting and hot and heavy. I guess that I didn't anticipate things being this weird between us today.

Although Ridge seems completely fine. It's only me who is acting like a stray, sketched-out kitten.

I'm not this girl. I'm bold and opinionated. I'm not bashful or dainty. And yet, right now, I can't even look this man in the eye because I'm so freaking timid.

As I start to head out of the kitchen to go to the bathroom, he calls behind me, "Do you want chocolate chips in your pancakes or plain?"

The moment the words leave Ridge's lips, I come to a stop under the archway that leads to the hall where the bathroom is. I stand there, frowning for a moment before I turn back toward him. I keep my clothes tight against my chest as I take in the sight of his back to me while he makes pancakes for our breakfast.

"Why are you making me pancakes?" I whisper.

He doesn't turn to face me right away, but continues to flip them over.

"I mean, I woke up hungry and wanted some," he says matter-of-factly. "Figured the nice thing to do would be to share them with the woman who had made me come so many times last night before I gave her a lift back to her place." He turns to face me, shrugging. "But if you've got something against pancakes, more for me, sweetheart."

I love pancakes. Plain and chocolate chip. But the thing is, I'm not even sure it's the pancakes I want as much as it is to sit at the table and chat with the man who made them. And that right there is an issue because I've already crossed the line of professionalism, and now, the more we drag this out, the more complicated it becomes.

Okay, that's an understatement. I took dynamite, and I blew up the freaking line altogether.

"The truce ended at midnight, remember?" I whisper. "I don't think people who hate each other eat pancakes together. Do you?" His face falls, but before he even has time to answer, I sigh. "I, uh, should probably change and get going. But it's not that far, so I think I'll walk."

His expression goes from bummed to aggravated. "It's fifteen degrees outside." He states the words almost like he's taunting me. "I'll give you a ride." His eyes narrow like he's challenging me. "But not until you eat a goddamn pancake."

"That wasn't the deal, Ridge," I growl quickly. "What are we even doing right now?"

Putting a few pancakes on two plates, he sets them down on the table. "We're eating breakfast, Fireball—that's what we're doing." He jerks his chin upward. "Go change, before they get cold."

Instead of arguing with him over why it's a bad idea for us to drag our time out together, I walk down the hallway, keeping my clothes in my arms. I can't stop wondering why he isn't just letting me go. And why he cares if I walk home when it's cold outside.

Him caring is making this whole thing messier than it already was.

Ridge

I turn down the driveway, not bothering to say anything to my passenger because it's obvious she doesn't want to talk. I had to practically force her to eat my pancakes, and I know they were good because I'd made sure not to burn them today.

The short drive to Stella's rental has been quiet and awkward as fuck. I knew, today, we'd go back to how we usually are, but how we usually are is more fun than whatever this shit is. She's quiet and acting nervous. She's fidgeting with her hands, and she's never struck me as someone who fidgets. I guess because she's always so confident.

Just before my truck comes to a stop in front of the house, I glance over at her. "What you said yesterday ..." I pause. "About Tucker."

"What about it?" she utters mindlessly.

"Would you really do that?" I press the brakes, shifting my truck into park. "You'd go to the one you think is the weakest link to try to get what you want?"

I expect her to leap from my truck like her ass is on fire, but instead, she turns toward me. Her eyes hold the same look in them that I saw at the tree farm yesterday. Only now, there's a hint of anger too. Yesterday, there was only sadness.

"Ridge, no offense, but some of us have to do shit for our work that we don't love. So, yes, if charming a client to get what I want, all while keeping my clothes on, is what it takes, I will absolutely do that." She looks out the window, nodding toward the ocean in front of the house. "I don't just ... get to live in a beautiful home. I have to work for what I have. And guess what. Because I have a thing called a vagina, I have to work twice as hard."

I know what she's trying to say. She sees our beautiful houses and ocean views and assumes that our lives are easy and that we've been given everything we have just because our family owns the wharf and the land our houses are on. But she couldn't be more wrong.

"Do you think I love waking up at three in the morning most days to go to work? Or do you think I enjoy the fact that I have to go to the chiropractor a few times a month just because my back is fucked up from breaking traps aboard for as many years as I have? What about the weeks or months when there are absolutely no fucking lobsters out there, and the price of bait and fuel is through the roof, but I know my bills aren't going to stop coming in the mail, and neither are my crew's?" I'm pissed now, and I don't even try to hide it. "And what about the rough days where I'm out there, constantly watching the two guys on the stern of my boat, worrying the worst will happen and it'll be my fault? Do you think that shit's easy?" I'm practically growling now. "I'll give you the answer. It's not. But this land? Knowing, one day, the next generation in our family will take this over and it'll keep being passed down? That's what makes it worth it."

I look straight ahead. "You're wasting your time, Stella. My family—Tucker included—will never give this up."

My jaw tenses as all the fun we had last night disappears, and all that's left is the hate for this woman who thinks she can insult us by coming here and throwing a check at us.

"My parents invited you to dinner to be nice, but there's no reason for you to stay anymore. You should pack your shit and get the fuck out of town. Before you've made an enemy of more than just me."

Now, I look over at her, holding her hazel eyes with my own. "Go home, city girl. You don't belong here." I should stop there, but I'm fucking mad. "Don't bother trying to seduce Tucker; you won't get anywhere with him. And besides, I had you the entire night, in every position possible, and I still would *never* so much as consider taking your deal."

"Fuck you," she hisses, eyes narrowing. "You know what I think?"

"Oh, I'm fucking dying to know."

"Maybe you just don't want me near your brothers," she snarls before smirking, getting back that annoying confidence that I picked up on the first few times we met. "I mean, after all, when Riley offered me a ride home, you put a stop to that real fast, didn't you?" She fucking smirks. "I don't think you hate me at all, Ridge Adams. In fact, I think you just hate how much you care what I do."

"Fuck you. That's the furthest thing from the truth," I snap. "I don't give a shit what you do or who you do it with."

My jaw tenses, and my nostrils flare. I wish I could tell her she's wrong and actually mean it, but the truth is, I do fucking care what she does. I care too damn much. But, fuck no, I'm not going to tell her that.

In the midst of my anger, my cock twitches. On one hand, there's something about her that I can't fucking stand, and on the other, it makes my dick hard.

"Keep telling yourself that, big guy." She winks. "You know, I was going to call my boss and tell him this was pointless and that I was ready to come back." She tsks me. "But then you had to go and say that thing about having me the entire night, and I decided, nah … I'm not ready just yet." She tilts her head to the side. "You see, sometimes, there're loopholes when it comes to getting what we want. Sometimes, it's finding the weakest link. But sometimes? It's finding a problem and bringing attention to it." She leans over slightly, continuing to smirk at me. "The property lines here seem awfully … unprofessionally done. Think I'll have a look into the assessment. You know, just to be sure everything here is legal."

When she turns away, I reach forward, gripping her chin. "Don't fuck with my family, Fireball. It won't end well for you."

The heartless-tough-girl act falters, and I see a look of shock in her eyes.

Pulling away from me, she glares. "I may just have to fuck with your brother," she whispers. "Or should I say … fuck your brother?"

The veins in my neck must bulge, and breathing becomes an actual fucking job. Everything inside of me wants to rush to the passenger side, throw her over my shoulder, carry her into the rental, and fuck her until she's screaming out my name again.

Because I don't want to even think about her screaming out anyone else's.

But I let her leave, and I don't even watch her as she walks away.

And despite how fucking angry I am, my cock stands tall.

Because that's what Stella does to me, and I hate it.

Chapter 12

Stella

"Obviously, he's the killer," I utter before taking a bite of my Toaster Strudel. "Even an idiot would know that."

After Ridge dropped me off and was a complete dick to me, prompting me to tell him I was going to fuck his brother, I took a long-ass shower in an attempt to wash him from my body, and then I put my pajamas on and haven't left the couch since. Well, other than to get some Cheetos or a fresh Toaster Strudel and pour a can of Coke over ice.

I'm supposed to call Victor soon, and I don't even know what I'm going to say. I might have told Ridge that I'd fuck with his family and their land, but I wouldn't actually do that. Despite him being an asshole, his family seems like good people. And I'm smart enough to know that I could offer them unlimited money and they'd still say no. Some things just can't be bought.

My phone vibrates, and I sigh when I see Victor's message, telling me to call him now. Taking my last bite, I take a swig of my soda and wash down the breakfast pastry before hitting Call. Most of my time here has been spent exploring the area, watching TV, or hating on Ridge Adams. I'm sure the company wouldn't be pleased to know that I have hardly worked at all, but that's why they aren't going to find out.

"Hoping for good news," he says, answering the phone. "Did you seal the deal yet, Stewart?"

Shit, he's really cutting right to the chase.

I cringe, chewing on my bottom lip.

"Uh, not exactly," I answer, attempting not to stutter. "Victor, I just don't think it's going to happen." I tell him the truth. It's something I've known since my first encounter with Ridge and his dad. I could see it all over their faces—this place is priceless to them. But I know I need to say something else. "I'm sorry."

He's silent for a second, and I know right away, that means he's pissed. Victor is a spoiled brat who isn't used to being told no. But what he has to realize is that he sent me on an impossible mission, and aside from drugging this family and then forging their signatures, it's not in the cards for Ironbound to buy and build here.

"And why is that?" His tone is less than impressed, but before I can answer, of course he has to add something. "I sent you because I thought you could handle this, Stella. Did I make a mistake?"

"They are never going to sell their land, Victor. I'm sorry. I know how big this would be for Ironbound, but we need to find something else." I pinch the bridge of my nose. "This family would go to war before they ever considered selling out."

"Then maybe a war is what they need," he tosses back, and instantly, the hairs on the back of my neck rise.

"What are you saying?" I whisper, standing up and pacing around the living room.

Victor cares about no one other than himself. That makes him a dangerous person to have working against you. And I fear that soon, the Adams family will know that.

"I'm saying that I've been around this business enough to know that when there's that much land, something has been done that wasn't by the book at some point in time. And we're going to find out what it was."

"You've been the CEO for, like, a year, Victor," I say, but I quickly change the subject, not wanting to make things worse. "What are you even saying? You're going to, what, blackmail them?"

"You know what I'm saying, Stella." He's almost hissing now. Not in the way a snake does, but like a twenty-four-year-old man who has been on his mother's tit since he was born. "And if I'm being honest with you, if you'll quit this easily on something, I'm not sure you're the right fit for us anymore."

Pompous motherfucker.

Thoughts of being homeless again flash through my mind, and even though I've done nothing but pig out all day, I almost feel that hunger in my stomach from when I was a kid with no money to buy a snack and no parents to care if I had one. I can't lose this job. So, even though I want to call him a douchebag and tell him to pound sand, I'm not in a position to piss him off. Not yet anyway. Someday, I'll have enough money that I won't need to take his shit, but until I'm ready to start my own company, I need to lie low. So, instead of ruffling any more feathers, I exhale.

"No, I'm not giving up. I just … I didn't want to be here, wasting money and time on a project that will never happen." I plop down on the couch, dragging my hand down my face. "I'll see what I can find."

"I knew you wouldn't let me down," he says, suddenly chipper. "We'll have you back home before Christmas—even if you're flying back Christmas Eve!" He barks out a laugh, and before I can tell him that I don't care if I fly home on Christmas Eve or Christmas Day, he says, "Talk soon!"

When he ends the call, a sick feeling fills my gut because I know that no matter what, something bad will happen. I'll either lose my job or I'll have a hand in the Adams losing what they love most.

And despite Ridge's hurtful words, I really don't want that.

Ridge

"Wind is gonna gust up to thirty knots tomorrow, you know," Jake says as we finish loading bait on for tomorrow. "Guess the sea is supposed to build to eight-foot swells by noon."

I slam around a few crates, irritated that this is at least the fifth thing he's mentioned today about tomorrow's weather being shit. I know that means he doesn't want to go, but that sucks to be him because he's going anyway.

"Well, we haven't been in almost a week, and we've got to get out one more time before Christmas because that always fucks up the schedule," I grumble. "The weather isn't supposed to turn until afternoon, so that's the point of leaving at one a.m. instead of three thirty tomorrow. Get out, get in, call it a day."

"Jake is just being a little bitch," Connor says, popping around the corner. "Ain't nothing we can't handle. Especially on this bad bitch." He pats his hand against the washboard of the boat.

I'm in a terrible mood today. Just like I have been the past three days. I keep trying to tell myself it's just the stress of winter fishing, but I've been pissy ever since the last encounter I had with Stella, when I dropped her off at her place and she told me she was going to fuck my brother. Since then, I've tried to keep all my brothers busy with work around the wharf so they are never free because, fuck no, I'm not letting them near her.

Through the woods this morning, I could still see Stella's car at the rental house. But with Christmas being three days away, I don't understand why she's still here.

We set the last barrel of bait in the boat, and I move some shit around before tossing new bait bags into the bait box.

"Be here by one in the morning," I say. "Go get some rest. It's gonna come early."

"Aye, aye, Captain!" Connor calls out.

Meanwhile, Jake sighs. He hates getting up earlier than normal, and I can't blame him. Our normal time is early for most people, but leaving an hour after midnight? It downright sucks.

I hate hauling in the middle of the night, but I need to make my guys a paycheck, and I also need to tend to my shit. So, this one time, we all need to suck it up and do it.

Besides, it'll keep me busy so I'm not tempted to go see a certain mean redhead who I can't seem to get off my mind.

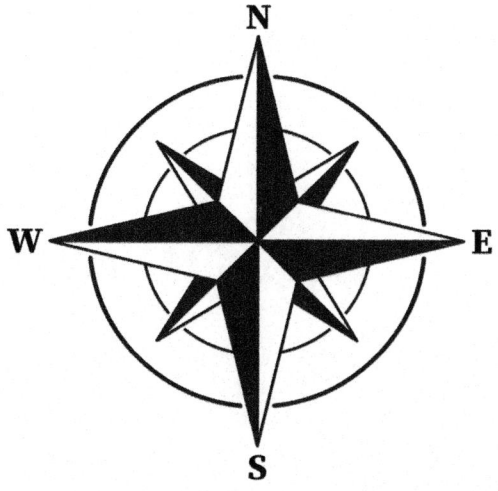

Chapter 13

Stella

"THANK YOU FOR MEETING ME," I say, holding my hot cup of coffee in my hands, looking across the table at Mrs. Adams. "I really appreciate it."

Katherine smiles, nodding. "Of course. Though I feel like I owe you a thank-you for distracting me today. I hate when the boys go out when it's rough. And I really hate it when they leave so early that it's basically night. But do you know what I hate the most?"

I frown, not knowing what she's talking about. "What?"

"I hate when only one of them goes out." She shakes her head. "It's not safe not to have another boat nearby on rough, cold days. And so that's three different things that I hate that my son has decided to pull today."

"I don't—" I stop, still not following all the way. "Which one?"

She gives me a look and rolls her eyes. "Ridge, of course. My child who is as stubborn as a goddamn bull. He left at one a.m., which means he's got to be wiped out by now, and he still isn't in yet."

It shouldn't bother me, thinking about Ridge being out there on a day it's not nice out. He was rotten to me the last time we saw each other. And even if he hadn't been, we don't even get along. Well, aside from the one day we got along a little too well and then ended up having sex all night.

"Oh, wow." I take a sip from my coffee. "That's not good. I don't blame you for being worried."

When the fearful expression on her face intensifies, I set my cup down to reach across the table and pat her hand. "But he's been fishing for most of his life, right? So, I'm sure he'll be fine. Besides, he seems like the ... extremely cautious type to me."

She sighs, relaxing slightly. "Yeah. You know what? You're right. I'm being dramatic. That boy always has a plan for a plan. He'll be fine." Though

I can tell she's still worried, she attempts to give me a relaxed smile. "So, what was it you wanted to see me for?"

I've spent days thinking about the last conversation I had with Victor. Something in his voice told me that he wouldn't stop pushing until the Adams' property was his. Despite my desire to climb the ladder at work so that I can gain more experience, I genuinely don't want anyone to come between this family and their legacy. In a way, I envy what they have here. It's rare, and they don't deserve to have it threatened or taken away. Because of that, I knew I had to meet her today.

"I know that no amount of money would ever convince your family to sell out," I tell her genuinely. "I think I realized that right off the bat." I chuckle. "Ridge makes it pretty obvious how he feels."

"He does. With every single thing in life really." The corner of her lips turns up. "That boy sure loves his home and everything his family has built here."

"I know," I whisper. "And despite my … mixed feelings about your son, I admire the loyalty all of you have to something you clearly care so deeply about." I stop, looking down. "Which is why I needed to come here. To warn you …"

When I glance back up again, she's frowning. "What do you mean, warn me? What's that supposed to mean?"

I grimace inside, knowing that whatever I say, she'll still be wary of me because this entire thing is basically my fault. I know if I hadn't taken this opportunity, he would have offered it to someone far more ruthless than me. But Katherine isn't going to see it that way. In her eyes, I'll be the woman who came in and disrupted the peace and put her family's land at risk.

"Victor, my boss, is pretty convinced that with some digging, he'll be able to find something your family is hiding." I swallow sharply. "Something that'll make it easier for this land to go up for sale."

Confusion and shock are followed by anger, which covers every inch of her face, making her cheeks grow red.

"We have nothing to hide, I can assure you." She speaks sharply now, going into protective mode. "So, you can run back to your boss and tell him that if he's trying to scare us, it's not going to work."

She begins to slide toward the end of her seat to get up, but I reach for her hand.

"Katherine, wait," I say quickly. "I promise, I didn't think he'd do anything like this. If I did, I would have never come."

"But you did," she utters, looking at me with disgust. "Stay away from my family."

I pull my hand back, and she hurries to get up. Before I can say anything else, she grabs her coat and quickly rushes to the door. I could run after her and apologize again for my involvement, but I don't want to make it worse on her. Especially not when she's already concerned about her son.

So, instead, I sit here in this booth, staring straight ahead. Realizing that Christmas, a holiday she seems to love so much, is in two days. And here I am, ruining it for her. Just giving me another reason to hate this season that much more.

"You're shitting me," I mumble, creating a puff of smoke in the air from my breath because this car is so fucking cold. I turn the key again, squeezing my eyes shut and hoping for the best. "Come on, you stupid car. Don't take a giant shit on top of my already-shitty day."

The car won't start, and I inhale a deep breath, trying to calm myself before I have a full-on meltdown in this coffee shop parking lot and things get ugly. I don't need this today. This morning, I stubbed my toe. And then I found out my favorite Netflix series had been canceled. Twenty minutes ago, Katherine gave me a death glare and then walked out of the café. Now, my car won't start.

All of this shitty stuff, and it's not even Christmas yet.

Pushing the door open, I start toward the café to find the sign now says it's closed. "Amazing," I grumble, taking my phone from my pocket.

I could call Ridge. After all, I have his number, but something tells me he'd probably tell me to fuck off. And I don't know anyone else in the area—well, besides his family, and they sure as hell don't want to hear from me either. So, I suppose I'll call the closest garage and have it towed.

A loud exhaust startles me, and I look up to find a big white truck pulling into the parking lot, its windows so dark that I can't even see inside it. It parks, and for a moment, no one gets out.

Creeped out, I start toward my car just as the driver's door swings open and Riley steps out. He waves, flashing me that panty-dropping grin that I think is his signature smile before heading over.

"Hey, it's Stella, right?" he drawls, stopping next to my car where I stand.

I nod, knowing that his mom probably hasn't talked to him yet. If she had, he wouldn't be smiling that big at me right now.

"Thought so." He stops, his brow furrowing. "Everything all right? Why are you just standing outside your car? It's fucking cold out."

Despite the chill in the air, my cheeks heat up. Part of my issues from my shitty childhood that I carry with me is the inability to accept help. But right now, I'm not sure I really have a choice.

"Um, yes. I can't get the engine to turn over, so I'm going to call a tow truck." I shrug it off like it's all fine and dandy. "Not sure what's going on with the stupid thing."

Pulling the door open, he climbs behind the wheel and attempts to start it, and just like I could have told him would happen, it doesn't work.

"Well, it's not a dead battery—that much I know," he says thoughtfully, just as a gust of wind sweeps through the parking lot, sending some fallen snow spraying through the air.

I shiver, my lips trembling before I stuff my hands inside my pockets. Of course, Riley has to notice because, instantly, he waves toward his truck.

"My truck's warm inside. Let's go sit in there, and I'll call my friend Alex." He gets out of the car. "He owns a garage in town and has a tow truck. I'll have him come and grab it."

Guilt strikes me—because I know how angry his mom would be if she knew he was helping me out. Rightfully so too.

"You don't have to do that," I say, shaking my head. "If you give me the number, I can call."

Please don't help me. It only makes me feel worse.

"Hell no, I'm a gentleman." He winks before throwing his arm around me. "Come on. Let's get you out of the cold."

He smells different from Ridge, but delicious nonetheless. And yet, with his arm around me, I don't feel that same spark I did when it was his brother who was this close. Riley is an insanely attractive man who's clearly confident—as he should be. Yet, now that I've been *with* his brother, I can't get him off my mind, even with Riley so close.

Releasing his hold on me, he opens the passenger door, and I climb inside, thankful to be in the warm air, even though I know it's wrong for me to take advantage of how sweet he is after the mess I might have put his family in.

Once he closes the door, he jogs to the driver's side and climbs in before pulling out his phone. After a moment, he puts it to his ear.

"Yo, what's up?" He grins. "You hauling cars today or fucking off, like usual?"

He listens, his grin growing wider before he chuckles. "Hey, it's fucking blowing a fuck ton outside, so, hell no, I'm not out to haul."

His words make my stomach feel sick because if it's really that bad out today on the ocean, why on earth did Ridge go out?

Riley laughs again at whatever the dude on the other end of the line said. "Yeah, yeah, I bet."

He glances at me. "Hey, look, I have a friend whose car won't start, parked down here by Salt and Coffee. Is there any chance you can come get it?"

He listens for a few seconds. "All right, sounds good. We'll be right here."

Once the call ends, he hits a few buttons to turn off his own heated seat, but luckily, he leaves mine on.

"He'll be here in ten," he drawls. "Hopefully, you weren't here too long by yourself."

"No, only a few minutes," I answer softly. "Thank you for calling your friend." I smile. "And for letting me sit in your fancy, warm truck. Keyword: warm."

"It's not a problem." His deep voice is smooth, and every word packs a bit of flirtatiousness that Ridge doesn't have. "Been wondering where you've been. I noticed your car at the rental house, but haven't seen you." He eyes me over. "Where've you been hiding, girl?"

"Here and there, I suppose." I blush.

He just has a certain magnetism to him that makes me feel uncomfortable, although I also find it endearing at the same time.

"Are you staying here for Christmas?" he asks, obviously curious. And really, who could blame him?

It's clear that the holidays mean a lot to his family, and I'm sure it's strange that it's almost Christmas and I'm still here, poking around his land.

"Actually, I'm going to catch a flight home tomorrow night," I say truthfully.

A few minutes after Katherine left me sitting alone, I realized that I could no longer be a part of this thing between Victor and the Adams. I need to get out of here before shit hits the fan. Lucky for me, I found a flight home on Christmas Eve.

"There's supposed to be a snowstorm coming tomorrow. I hope your flight gets out," he says, seeming concerned. "I imagine you have family to get back and see."

He doesn't mean to hurt me with his assumption, but it does. Lucky for me, I have one helluva poker face, and I keep the pain hidden.

"Yeah," I say, selling it as best I can. "What about you? What're your big plans for Christmas?"

Even saying the word burns my throat, but I desperately need to take the attention from me and put it on him. And as sweet as he is, he seems like the type of guy who would love to talk about himself.

"Same as every year." He grins. "We go to my parents'. Mom makes way too much food. We play some card games, watch a movie, eat more food, and then call it a day."

He says it like it's no big deal, but in reality, I can't imagine what it would feel like to have that sort of stability, where you know that your family is going to get together for the holidays. And not only that, but you know your mom is going to do everything to make it special for you, even though you're a grown-ass man.

"Nice." I plaster on a polite smile.

Riley knows my reason for being here, yet he doesn't go out of his way to make sure I know he hates me. I'm not sure this guy could hate anyone though. Unlike Ridge, who is downright mean.

And really good in bed.

While we wait for the tow truck, Riley puts on some music, and I keep thinking that by tomorrow, I can put this entire trip to Maine in the past.

Forever.

Merry freaking Christmas to me.

Ridge

"That might have sucked, but it was worth it, boys," I say to the guys while they sit on the bench in the wheelhouse.

Both play on their phones like zombies, and between the three of us, I don't know if we have enough left in us to unload the lobsters we caught today.

"*Sucked* isn't the word for it," Connor says, yawning. "I don't even wanna drive home; I'm so tired."

"Drink another one of those girlie energy drinks; you'll be fine," I tease him, keeping my hand on the ship's wheel as I sit in the captain's chair.

Today was one of those rare days when there wasn't anyone else out. Typically, I don't like to put my crew in a position to be out on the ocean when there aren't any other boats around, but we really didn't have a choice. My brothers decided to be lazy, and I couldn't do that.

Besides, the guys don't know it yet, but when we get in, I'll give them their Christmas bonus. Though they probably do know it's coming because I do it every year.

Steaming into the bay, I've never been more excited to see my house from the water. As corny as it may sound, I always love looking up and seeing my house sitting among the trees. I think I like the view of our land from the boat more than anywhere else.

Taking a sip from my Monster, I yawn. It's been a long day. It's been windy as fuck, which means the sea has been building all day, making this sail into my wharf painfully long, and I'm beat.

Just like I have on the days out to haul ever since she's been here, I nonchalantly look at the house where Stella is staying. And every day her car is still there, I'm more surprised.

Only today … her car isn't there.

Instead, my fucking brother's truck is pulling in.

Riley, you motherfucker.

Chapter 14

Stella

I PULL MY LAPTOP OUT AND PLOP MYSELF ON THE COUCH. PULLING the screen up, I click on the Safari icon before typing in *oceanfront land for sale, Maine.*

Looking at property after property, I know they aren't big enough for what Ironbound plans to do, but I'm determined to find something—anything—that'll make Victor happy enough to leave Ridge's family alone.

Riley dropped me off not long ago, and though he offered to hang out longer, I made up an excuse that I needed to pack. It's not really a lie; eventually, I do need to pack. But I'll probably save it for tomorrow. I just didn't want to lead him on and have him thinking that I was interested in any way. As cute as he is and funny too … I'm just not into him.

The faint sound of a loud vehicle engine, followed by a door opening and slamming shut, sends me shooting upward and setting my laptop on the coffee table before rushing toward the window to see who's outside. I don't even make it to the glass to look before a pounding sounds from the door. But I can see through the curtain, and I'd know Ridge's profile anywhere.

Exhaling, I look upward and sigh before, finally, I step forward and pull the door open.

"Take it easy on the door, dickhead," I say, waving my hand toward the spot he was just pounding on. "I don't want to get charged for you denting it."

"If it's your dickface of a boss paying for this place, I'll rip the entire thing off the fucking hinges," he sneers before pushing his way past me and into the house.

"Um … yeah, sure. Come on in. Make yourself at home. Hey, want some tea?" I sass, shaking my head before slowly closing the door behind him.

When I turn around, he stands just a few feet away, looking at me.

"What are you doing here?" A putrid smell hits my nose, and I fight back a gag. "And what the hell is that smell?"

"I just got off the boat," he says, keeping his eyes on mine. "It's bait. Guess you wouldn't know that, would you, city girl?"

"Nope." I fold my arms over my chest. "Typically, I avoid rolling in bait and walking around. It's not good for my dating lifestyle," I deadpan. "And again, why are you here?"

"Why was Riley here?" His voice is cold—and dare I say, accusing, like he actually has any right to ask me that. "I saw his truck from the boat. What did you do, call him over for a business meeting in hopes he'd agree to sell to you?"

"Um, yes!" I nod frantically. "I figured if I gave him the world's greatest blow job, he'd see my side of things and then … bam! Done deal. Ladder climbed. Happy day!"

His face instantly reddens, not with embarrassment, but anger. His fists ball up at his sides, and his jaw tightens.

"That's an awful lot of reactions for someone who doesn't care," I say, leaning back against wall. "Or a guy who says he doesn't care at least."

"I care about this land," he snarls. "That's it."

"And so do I," I coo.

I could tell him the truth. That nothing happened between me and Riley and that I'm going to do everything I can to make Ironbound leave his family alone. I could say a lot of things to make him feel better, but after he walked in here, hotheaded and accusing me of the worst, I don't really want to make him feel better.

He takes a step closer, and I swear that smoke rolls off his body. Now, he hovers over me, glaring down.

"Did you really suck my brother's dick, Stella?" He slaps his palm against the cupboard above my head.

I glare back, angry because it's none of his business. I could say yes and hurt him, but for whatever reason, I can't bring myself to do it.

"No, asshole," I say through gritted teeth. "I would never give some-one a blow job to close a deal. I was being sarcastic."

His chest continues to heave, but I watch him sigh in relief. His gaze sweeps over my face, dropping to my lips, and my body grows weaker as I drag in a few shallow breaths of my own.

He could kiss me right now, and I wouldn't tell him to stop. He could tear my clothes off, and I'd probably help him. But something tells me that's not going to happen.

"I have to go," he breathes out. "And you should go back to New York."

"Don't worry, Outlaw. Tomorrow night, I'll be gone," I whisper, feeling my heart beating out of my chest.

I want him to kiss me. I want him to push me up against the kitchen counter and have his way with me.

After he showers the smell off him, of course.

He doesn't do either of those things though. Instead, he swallows shallowly. "I have to go," he mutters before slowly backing away from me.

When he gets back to the door, his hand lingers on the knob. "Have a safe flight back, Stella. And don't come back. You'll never get what you're looking for."

Within seconds, he's gone. And I'm hit with the realization that this was likely the last time I will ever see Ridge Adams.

And like so many other times before, he's leaving me clenching my damn thighs together.

Ridge

Fuck, I wanted to kiss her mouthy lips.

Right when she confirmed she didn't suck Riley's dick, I wanted to shove her down onto her knees and force my cock so far down her throat that her eyes were rolling back while she choked on me. Because that's the punishment she deserves for even saying that she had his cock in her perfect mouth.

This anger inside of me, it's rooted so deep. And the roots, they continue to grow, wrapping around every single part of my being, making me an even angrier son of a bitch than before.

I can't be trusted to be alone with that girl because every time I am, I can hardly keep my hands off her. I know she's not right for me, yet when I saw my little brother's truck there, I raced over to see what the fuck had happened between them. And I know damn well it doesn't have a thing to do with land and everything to do with not wanting Stella to be with anyone else.

I pull in front of my house and kill my truck engine. Throwing my head back, I groan loudly.

Once she's back in New York, life will go back to normal.

That may be true, but until then, I have to try not to kill my own brother.

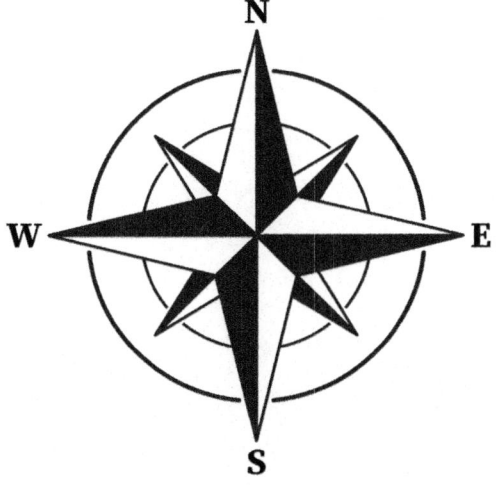

Chapter 15

Stella

THE AIRPORT IS A GHOST TOWN, BUT I'D PREFER THIS TO THE alternative. My flight isn't due to take off for another five hours, but when it started spitting snow in Holiday Harbor, I panicked that the roads would be a mess if I waited until the afternoon to leave. I guess I forgot to take into consideration that this airport is tiny, and there's only one restaurant, a small shop, and a place to get snacks and coffee.

Self-serve coffee . . . ew.

I may go through multiple packs of Toaster Strudels a week and love Coke, but when it comes to coffee, hell yes, I am a snob. I want the steamed milk. I want the cold foam. And I even want the sprinkled cinnamon on top. Give me it all.

I look out one of the large windows and cringe as I watch the heavy snow blowing around the runway. As the night goes on, the wind is supposed to pick up, and the snow is going to get heavier.

All day, I hoped that my plane would take off before the worst weather hit. Now, I'm worried about two scenarios happening. One, the runway is snowy and windy, and our plane either skids right off it during takeoff or gets blown over, and of course . . . I die. Or two, they cancel my flight, and I'm forced to stay in Maine even longer than I already have.

My phone vibrates, and when I pull it out, my eyes bug out of my head when I read the message from the airline that my flight is being delayed.

Until December *freaking* 27.

That means, for three more nights, I'm stuck in Maine. Unless I can find another airline provider, but it's not like I want to put more money into a flight that may not happen. After all, the cost didn't come out of Ironbound's pocket, but my own.

Victor has no idea I'm coming back to The Big Apple empty-handed because I haven't told him that I'm heading back yet. I figured I'd show up and pull out all the amazing properties I'd found that he could buy up, salvaging my job. Sounds so much better than doing it over the phone.

Or it did, before I got stuck here.

I look up at the few people scattered throughout the airport, all looking at their phones with sad expressions on their faces. It's Christmas Eve, and I am sure that, unlike me, they all have loved ones they want to get home to.

I have a few good friends who will wish me merry Christmas, but aside from that, I'm on my own.

As I see a couple heading toward the exit, it hits me. I need to book a hotel. And fast. After all, how many could there possibly be?

"You have got to be kidding me," I say, caught somewhere between being angry and panicking as I look at every single hotel listing, saying they have no availability until the day after Christmas.

Tossing my phone in the seat beside me, I drag my hand down my face.

The roads are undoubtedly awful. There are no hotels to stay in nearby. And there's no way I can sleep in one of these uncomfortable chairs in this airport.

Glancing at my phone, I sigh. There's only one person I know who I can call and he'll come get me right now and not make me feel bad. The same guy who gave me his number yesterday in case I needed a ride to pick my car up. Fortunately for Riley, he didn't have to because the mechanic was nice enough to deliver it right to my rental house. Perks of him thinking I was friends with Riley, I suppose.

Snatching my phone, I hit the name on my screen and bring it to my ear while I wait for him to answer.

Riley ... the man who is going to be my hero again.

Ridge

This feeling that's flowing through my body, making me irritated as fuck, is foreign. At least, it was until Stella Stewart landed in Holiday Harbor and turned me into *this* guy.

The kind of guy who wants to punch his own brother on Christmas

Eve while we're supposed to be hanging out, playing cards with our parents, because even though she said nothing had happened between them, I know he had wanted something to happen. Why else was he at her fucking house?

"I don't get it. Why did she call you?" I say, following Riley down the hallway. "She has my number too."

"I don't know, dickface. All that matters is she called someone." He pauses. "Or maybe she has the hots for me. Who knows?"

I shoot him an icy glare. "No, she doesn't."

And as he starts to pull his jacket on, I do the same, and my mom throws her arms up, coming to the mudroom.

"Where are you going? It's a mess out there!" she yells. "I hope you don't plan on driving anywhere. I swore I heard you say the airport, but I must have heard you wrong, Riley, because I didn't raise a complete idiot."

After pulling his shoes on, he leans forward and kisses our mom on the cheek. "I have to go get a friend who is stranded at the airport, Mom. I'll be careful."

"Like hell you are! There have been multiple accidents already, and it's only going to get worse." She looks at me. "Tell him, Ridge."

"Can't," I say quickly. "Because I'm going too."

"What in the hell is wrong with you two?" Then she roars at my dad, who is, no doubt, still in his recliner, "Honey! Tell the boys to stop being stupid!"

"Stop being stupid," Dad calls back, too lost in his show to know why we're being stupid.

As Tucker steps into view, she throws her arms up toward him. "Don't tell me you're going too, Tuck. You're my smart one."

"Going where?" he says, confused.

Suddenly, Easton appears beside him. "I overheard Riley in the kitchen. He's going to go pick up that hot property girl at the airport." In true Easton form—as he's also known as the shit stirrer—he smirks. "Though I don't know why Ridge is going. Think he's got the hots for her."

"I don't have the hots for her," I say quickly. "I hate her."

"That's what they all say," Easton teases, grinning stupidly at us.

Throwing my arm around my mom, I give her a half hug.

"I'm sorry. We'll be safe though." I glance at Riley, narrowing my eyes. "I'm driving, so that should make everyone feel better."

His mouth hangs open. "What the fuck does that mean?"

Releasing my mom, I step forward and pull the door open and ignore him.

"Let's go," I mumble, not knowing why I'm so hell-bent on going.

Why does the thought of her sitting in that airport, all alone during a storm, make me feel like shit?

Why can't I just let my little brother be her hero?

And the biggest question of all: *Why do I have to step in?*

Who fucking knows?

Riley is quiet in the passenger seat, just like he has been the entire ride. We should have been at the airport twenty-five minutes ago, but because of the terrible road conditions and low visibility, we're not there yet.

He's played on his phone, but Riley isn't usually the type to be quiet, so I know something is wrong. And because I'm the asshole that I am, I can't bring myself to just ask him what it is. But I'm not stupid. I know it has to do with Stella and me demanding to drive to get her.

"Can you just say whatever it is you need to and get it out now?" I finally blurt out. "The whole silent treatment is annoying me."

"I don't know what you're talking about," he says in a less than convincing tone.

But I know Riley, and he isn't going to stop at that. He'll spill his guts. That's how he is.

"Why would it bother me that my control-freak big brother had to invite himself to come with me to pick up the girl I like, but also … didn't even trust me to fucking drive?"

His words hurt to hear because he just admitted he likes her. I like her too. But unlike my little brother, I'm too much of a stubborn prick to just admit it out loud.

"I've had my license for four years longer than you have, Ry. I just thought it would be better if I drove."

The truck slides a little on the snowy roads, but I straighten it out. My knuckles are fucking white from gripping the steering wheel so tightly, and once I have two passengers in here, I'll no doubt be more stressed than I already am. I'm not worried about me losing control of my truck; I'm worried about someone else on the roads doing that and hitting us.

When the conditions are this terrible, I suppose one good thing is, there's really no way for anyone to be driving fast. So, even if they did hit us, it would be low impact.

"Why were you so hell-bent on coming tonight?" Riley asks the question, and I don't even know how to answer it.

Stella is a city girl. I'm a fisherman who only leaves Maine in the winter for a month or so. I like the quiet of my town while she thrives in the city that never sleeps. Even if I do like her, what would be the point of telling anyone? It would never work.

"I just …" I pause. "I didn't want you on the road alone, I guess."

He's silent for a moment, but with his next words, I can almost hear his smirk. "That would be nice and all, if only it were true." He sighs. "You like her too, huh?"

I chew my cheek awkwardly. Riley loves women. He loves flirting with them, loves dating them, and even though he's had a lot of relationships, he's that guy who somehow always ends things on good terms. Because how the fuck do you get mad at a guy like Ry?

Me? I used to sleep around a bit. I've had a few short-term girlfriends, but I can never stand anyone to stick around too long.

And I've never been the jealous kind.

Until now.

"I don't know," I mumble. "I can't stand her most of the time. But every now and then …" I stop, feeling like a pathetic loser for what I'm even saying. "Not to mention, she came here to try to buy up our land. That land means everything to me."

"It does to all of us." Riley says the words like a statement. "Wait … the night you gave her a ride home, did you …"

"Not that night," I say, hoping he'll connect the dots and back the fuck off her once he realizes that I've been with her.

I made her scream out my name; she'll never scream out his that way.

I fucking hope anyway.

"So, you've already been with her," Riley mutters, and I might not be able to look at him, but I'm sure he's hanging his head. "I wish I had known that before I brought myself on this long-ass ride to the airport. Because if your dick has been near her, there's no fucking way I'm interested. I'm not Jeremiah."

"Jeremiah?" I ask. "Who the hell is that?"

"It's a show I watch. Too complex for you." He pauses. "Now that I think about it, you're Conrad. But still … no way in hell am I Jeremiah. I consider myself more of a Steven really."

Riley has always loved a lot of the same shows our mom does, and he also loves pop music. He once went to a Taylor Swift concert and raved about it to other fishermen over the radio for days. So, hard to say what this show is that he's talking about. All I know is, I'm not sure what my being Conrad means, but I have a feeling he's a dick.

And the closer we get to the airport, the more I keep thinking how I shouldn't have even come. I don't know what I'm expecting to gain here, and yet … here I am.

Stella

When Riley texts me that he's here, I'm not surprised at all when he walks through the airport doors. What is surprising—no, actually, what sends me into full-on shock mode is when Ridge walks in behind him. His eyes instantly find mine, and my stomach does that stupid thing it always does when he's close by. Despite the fact that he's a dick, he still gives a girl butterflies like no other.

Trudging toward them, I wheel my bag behind me.

"I'm so sorry that I had to make you come all the way here. I'm sure it was an awful ride. Thank you so much," I say, stopping in front of Riley and giving him a hug. "But I had returned my rental car, and there's literally no motels nearby to stay at, so my only option is to go back to the rental house."

"Don't even worry about it." Riley smiles, but there's a hint of sadness in his eyes that I don't understand.

When I release him, I find Ridge's stare on me, and his blue eyes are swirling with anger. I suppose I should hug him, too, but I'm not going to do that. Hell no. With Riley, it's a friendly hug. If I hug Ridge, I'll end up dry-humping him.

Ridge steps around his brother and takes the suitcase from me.

In true mysterious Ridge Adams form, he jerks his chin toward the door. "We should go. It's only going to get worse out there."

And as he starts toward the exit with Riley and me following close behind, I exhale. All I know is, I came here, trying to make a big move that would make my boss and coworkers notice me and give me some credit, but now, I'm going rogue, no longer giving a shit about closing this deal and also spending an inappropriate amount of time with the people who are supposed to be our potential sellers.

I dare to say, I've completely sunk my career. Or at least my career at Ironbound.

Chapter 16

Ridge

I STARE UP AT THE CEILING, MY EYES FEELING GRAVELLY BECAUSE I only got a few hours of sleep.

Merry fucking Christmas.

We dropped Stella off at her rental house just before midnight. Everything inside of me screamed to demand she stay with me in case the rental lost power, but seeing as she had spent the entire ride chatting with Riley and ignoring me, I didn't bother. So, for the entire night, I lay here, wondering if she'd lost power because the wind had been whipping so fiercely.

But now, it's Christmas, and I can't stand the thought of her being all alone. So, despite my mixed feelings, I'm going to ask my mother if she can come to Christmas at my parents' house.

I don't believe in instant love. I think it's complete bullshit. Yet ever since I spent that day with Stella, I can't get her off my mind. But even if she wasn't here in hopes I'd sell out, we live two different lives. She's a city girl. She'd never slum it on the coast of Maine with me, a fisherman who spends his days off from the boat working at the wharf.

I want her so fucking bad again. I want to throw her on my bed and bury my face between her thighs, making her come so many times that she's begging me to stop by the end of it. But having her again will make this feeling inside of me grow more.

For whatever reason, she doesn't seem too fond of Christmas. So, with any luck, she'll decline when I ask her to come spend Christmas with my family. But I have to at least offer because if not, I'll feel like a heartless dick.

Looking at the time, I see it's after seven. My mom is for sure up and at it. No doubt preparing the insane amount of food she makes for Christmas every year.

Grabbing my phone from the nightstand, I decide to call her now to give her plenty of notice that I may bring Stella with me.

"Merry Christmas, babe!" she answers on the second ring. "How did you sleep?"

"Like shit," I mumble, but then remind myself that it's my mom's favorite day of the entire year and I need to be nicer. "Hey, I was wondering, would you mind if Stella came today?" Suddenly, I'm so nervous that I shoot out of bed, pacing my room. "She just … she doesn't have anywhere to go, and I'd feel like a dick if I didn't—"

"I'll stop you before you talk yourself to death because you feel nervous, telling me you like this girl." She laughs. "Riley already asked me, and I said yes. He's going to pick her up."

So much for not wanting her anymore.

"Of course he did," I drawl. "Well, I guess I'll see you in a bit then."

"Ridge, I do want to tell you the same thing I told Ry." There's concern in her voice, putting me on edge. "The company she works for is digging to find a reason for us to have to forfeit our land. So, while I agree that we can't let her spend Christmas alone, we can't trust her. At least not yet."

"Did she tell you that?" I slap my hand against the wall and look out the window at where my boat is sitting on its mooring.

"Yeah, she did." She sighs. "For what it's worth, I do think she feels bad."

"Yeah, I bet she does," I huff out. "All right, well, see you soon."

Once we both hang up, I narrow my gaze at the wooded area in the distance, toward where she's staying. I knew I couldn't trust her, and yet I sort of did anyway.

Heading toward the bathroom, I walk inside and turn on the shower. Because if I'm going to be able to stay pissed at her tonight, I need to fuck my hand first so that my dick doesn't get confused when she does something as simple as lick her plump lips.

Pulling my briefs down, I step into the water, wasting no time in gripping my cock and squeezing my eyes shut. I grunt when the image of Stella kneeling before me with water showering down on her flashes in my mind.

"Make it up to me," I grit out to absolutely no one. "Show me how sorry you are for being a conniving bitch."

I picture her biting her lip, soaked from the shower just before her lips part, and she leans forward, taking my cock into her hot mouth. I shiver when I feel myself sliding against her tongue. I could go slow and let her suck me how she wants, but she doesn't deserve that. So, instead, I imagine grabbing a fistful of her hair and yanking her head back enough to force her eyes on mine. Keeping her steady by her hair, I thrust my hips toward her, fucking her mouth with absolutely no remorse.

"That's right. Take it, slut," I growl, knowing how fucking insane I am right now, talking to myself in my shower.

I slap my hand against the wall, and I stroke my dick harder. I imagine fucking her mouth so hard that her eyes water because she's gagging, and I don't even let up because I know she doesn't want me to. No, something tells me she'd like it rough like that.

Swallow me down.

I feel my balls tighten, and I fight back a groan as cum begins to explode from my cock. Even though it's covering my hand, I imagine it's going down her throat, and she takes every drop like it's a fucking gift.

My head is spinning, and I keep a palm against the shower to steady myself. When my eyes finally open and the image of her on her knees before me is gone, I realize that it doesn't matter how many times I fuck my own hand, thinking about this woman …

It'll never get her out of my head.

Chapter 17

Stella

I'VE HAD A LOT OF STRANGE CHRISTMASES, BUT THIS ONE, HANDS freaking down, takes the cake. The food is delicious, just like I figured it would be when I first got the invite from Riley earlier, but after what had happened at the coffee shop, I know that Katherine doesn't trust me. She and Mathew have been polite yet a tad cold. And Ridge? Well, he won't even look my way.

Ridge's dog, Marlin, on the other hand, is going around the table, begging whoever he thinks he can get a table scrap from. I must look like the weakest link because he's been sitting at my feet for about ten minutes now, snorting in true Marlin fashion. Every now and then, I reach down and scratch his head, but then he always ends up begging even more.

"So, Stella …" Katherine addresses me for the first time this entire dinner, and suddenly, I'm nervous.

She's as intimidating as they come, even though she doesn't try to be. She's just … tough. Unlike myself, who could never thrive here.

"Yeah?" I say, wiping my mouth with my napkin before setting it down in front of me.

"Did your flight get rescheduled?"

"It did. I'm flying out on the twenty-seventh now." I pause, not wanting her to think I'm purposely staying here a few extra days just to spend time with her boys. "That was the earliest they could do."

"The storm made quite a mess of the airport." Mathew finally speaks now. "Most grounded flights I've ever seen in Maine."

"Yeah, it was pretty wild, that storm," I answer politely and honestly.

"Well, I'm sorry that you weren't able to get home for Christmas Day." Katherine not only sounds genuinely sympathetic, but looks it too. "I'm sure you have friends and family who are missing you for the holidays. Maybe you can do a late celebration with them."

Despite my best efforts, everything inside of me freezes because I don't know how I'm going to respond to this. I open my mouth to throw something back—anything that'll make her believe that I do have a family or loved ones.

Or a plant that loves me. Anyone. Anything.

Nothing comes out, and my cheeks begin to redden. The more seconds that pass while I try to come up with something to say, the faster my heart beats in my chest. But before I can die of humiliation and fall under the table, Ridge's deep voice cuts through the room sharply. And even though I know he's about to be an ass, I welcome it.

"Will that be before or after you take whatever it is you've dug up on our land to your dickhead boss?" Ridge's voice isn't loud right now, but it still rattles my bones. "What did you find anyway? We're all dying to know."

When I look into Ridge's eyes, I can see the anger. But I also feel a sense of something else. Sympathy maybe? Pity perhaps? Maybe I'm crazy for thinking this way, but something inside me tells me that even though he's angry and he wants all those answers, he was also trying to save me from answering his mom. Because after we went to the tree farm and he found out a bit about why I didn't celebrate Christmas, I'm sure he knows that no one is waiting for me back home.

"Ridge, cut the shit," Riley warns him.

"Wait, what?" Easton looks around the table. "What is he talking about?"

As much as I hate to admit it, I'd rather have them all look at me like I'm an awful human and scream at me about business-related shit than talk about Christmas and why I hate it as much as I do.

While everyone else demands answers, Tucker, per usual, says nothing. He just sits in his seat, observing his family. But when I look at him, even he looks at me kind of weird instead of his bashful self.

Even he sees through my bullshit now.

"What the hell is going on?" Easton keeps a fork in his fingers, pressed against the plate of food that I think is his third, but his eyes sweep the table intensely.

"Yeah, someone fill us in." Tucker's voice is stern and angry. "What the hell did *she* do?"

Out of all of them being mad at me, for some reason, Tucker hits me the hardest. Which makes no sense because I haven't spent any time with him. Hell, I've only heard his voice a few times, and he's never actually spoken to me. But during the times when Ridge was being an ass, I'd always look across the table and find Tucker's face with absolutely no judgment on it. Now, it quite possibly holds the most.

Katherine's face flashes with sympathy, but she sighs. "Perhaps you should just take the floor, Stella," she whispers. "That way … it's all out there."

Before I even answer, Mathew is reaching in front of me, filling my glass with wine. When my eyes meet his, he gives me a subtle nod of reassurance. I don't know why on earth he'd help me out right now, but for whatever reason, he is.

Taking the glass, I take a long swig, hoping it'll settle my nerves. When that doesn't happen, I realize I'm on my own here. Every single person at this table deserves to know the truth—just how shady of a person the man I work for can be.

"When I was sent here to talk to you all, I was told you owned a large amount of waterfront property, and we had big plans for it if we could get you to sell," I say honestly and evenly. "Not long after I arrived, I learned that I'd have better luck winning the Powerball than I ever would at convincing this family to part with their land—no matter what the number on the check was."

My eyes find Ridge's, and I can tell he's hanging on my every word. His eyes aren't angry, but inquisitive.

"The other day, I informed my boss that it was time to look at other properties, that this was a dead end. With my whole entire heart, I know this land means everything to you all, and I knew I needed to give up any idea or fantasy I had of closing this deal for Ironbound." I sigh, cringing. "And let's just say, my boss didn't want to hear that." I chew my lip, looking down at my plate.

"From the time his spoiled ass came into this world, Victor Johnson has never been told no, and when I told him my thoughts, he started to talk crazy and say things that indicated he believed he could find a loophole to get your land."

"Loophole?" Easton says. "What kind of loophole?"

My eyes move to Mr. Adams. "He thinks that with an oceanfront property so large, at some point, something wasn't done legitimately. He really thinks that if we dig up enough dirt, we'll find something shady."

I don't know what I expect him to do. Flinch maybe? Because in my experience, everyone has something to hide. And perfect families like this one are often not as flawless as they may seem. But instead of looking uncomfortable or shifting in his seat, Mathew looks ... relaxed.

"He can dig all he wants. He isn't going to find anything." He lifts his fork, taking a bite of casserole. "That's damn good, hon."

"Mathew," Katherine scolds him, "didn't you hear what she said? How can you be so sure?"

He takes a sip of his drink before setting the glass back down on the wood table. "Because I'm not stupid. I knew the day would come when some asshole showed up, trying to take what was ours." He stops, waving his hand toward me. "Not you, Stella. You're not the asshole."

"She kind of is," Ridge utters, earning him a glare from both of his parents.

"Anyway, we have nothing to worry about." He shrugs. "So, you can all calm the hell down and enjoy Christmas."

My eyes stay on him. "You're sure?" I whisper. I swear to God, I feel like I could cry tears of relief right now. "Because I'm telling you, he's ruthless. So is his dad."

Setting his fork down, he wipes his mouth. "Stella, this land is the most important thing to this family, besides each other. So, yes, I'm sure there is absolutely nothing about the land or us that your scumbag piece-of-shit boss is going to dig up."

It takes a moment to digest, but eventually, I sigh in relief. Ever since my phone call that day with Victor, I've been sick to my stomach, thinking that something was going to happen to this land. Before I met this family, maybe I wouldn't have cared. But now? I can't even fathom it because they are all genuine, good people. I suppose I should never have assumed that they ever did anything shady to get this land because that's not who they are. This family has values and integrity.

Unlike my boss.

The celebration in my head is short-lived because, of course, Ridge is instantly back to firing questions my way. He hasn't trusted me since I landed here. So, why on earth would he start now?

"And were you a part of it?" He swallows. "The digging to find something that would hopefully put us in hot water or take us out?"

"Absolutely not," I tell him truthfully, not faltering for a split second. "Victor thinks I'm still here in Maine, trying to get you to sell. But the truth is, I stopped trying to get you to sell basically the night I came here for dinner the first time." I nervously run my finger up and down the chilled glass, not looking at Ridge or anyone else. "I stopped *wanting* you to sell out not long after that too."

My eyes skim the table for a moment, and I find everyone is seemingly satisfied with my answer. But while everyone else seems to relax and go on talking about something else, Ridge's eyes stay on mine. But there's not anger in them anymore.

No, it's something else. Something I can read like a book when it comes to him because it's exactly how he looked at me that night in his kitchen—moments before he had my legs spread wide while I lay back on his countertop.

The look in his eyes? It's need. Desperate, agonizing need.

And I recognize it instantly because it's exactly what I'm feeling too.

Ridge

Home Alone plays, and my dad snores loudly in his recliner, just like he does every year after all the Christmas shit is over. Tucker and Easton left a few minutes ago. And my mom is working on knitting something in the corner because she's suddenly decided in the past few weeks, she's a knitter. I'd tease her about it, but this is what she always does. She's constantly finding a new hobby that she wants to start. Some she's good at, and others ... not so much.

Tonight, my family got to see the playful side of Stella that I had gotten to see on the day we went to the tree farm. She let her guard down, and she genuinely smiled. But now, she's exhausted. I've been watching her fight sleep for the past twenty minutes, and her eyes finally flutter shut. Within a few seconds, she's out like a light with Marlin curled up beside her.

With Riley across from me, he stirs slightly, sitting up a bit, and I can sense instantly that he's going to say something.

"You should give her a ride home," he drawls, leaning forward, shrugging his shoulders. "You're my big brother, and I've never seen you give a shit about what a girl is doing." He jerks his chin toward where Stella sleeps. "With her though, you care."

My eyes shift from him to her before moving back to him. "I hardly know her," I huff out, trying to play it off like he's not right. Like this girl hasn't consumed my every fucking thought after I spent one night with her. "She could still be here to fuck with us, you know."

"Yeah, okay." He shakes his head, standing up. "We both know that isn't true. But either way, I'm headed out. Merry Christmas, you grumpy fucker."

My mom comes out from the kitchen. "Are you taking off, Ry?" And when he nods, she walks toward him, wrapping her arms around his body. "Merry Christmas, babe. I love you."

"Love you too. Thanks for everything." He hugs her back. "As usual, you made Christmas great for all of us. Even if we are grown-ass men."

"Well, you could be sixty, but you all will still be my babies." She gives him one last squeeze before stepping back. "Get home safe, babe. That storm left a damn mess."

He salutes her before heading out to drive himself the whopping quarter of a mile he has to go. But still, she worries, I'm sure.

My dad snores so loud that he startles himself awake, and my mom looks at me and giggles before she walks over to him and pats his shoulder.

"Time to go to bed, love."

Groggily, he stands up and holds his hand up to me. "Merry Christmas, Ridge." He yawns and leans in to kiss my mom. "I'll be in bed, waiting for my Christmas present."

She swats at his chest but blushes, and I grimace.

"That's just gross," I grumble, pushing myself from the couch. "Think I'll head out too."

My mom and I both look down at Stella, and I run my hand over the top of my head.

"I'll get her." I shrug. "Night. Love you."

After hugging me tightly and turning off the TV, she heads off to bed, but not without Marlin hot on her heels.

She smiles down at him, then looks back at me. "Can my grandboy stay the night? It's Christmas."

"Go ahead. He farts all night, so you have at it." I chuckle, and within seconds, she's walking down the hallway with him right beside her.

That dog loves two things in life: sleeping and eating. And I'm honestly not sure which one he loves more.

Once everyone is gone, I stare nervously down at Stella, not wanting to make her feel awkward when I lift her up to take her out to the car.

She's so pretty this way. Sound asleep and seeming peaceful. Her skin is almost porcelain, and her lips are a deep pink. But even though she's beautiful right now, there's just something about her mouthy lips that makes me love them more when she's awake.

Kneeling down, I slide my arm behind her and lift her into my arms before standing. She stays asleep, nudging her cheek against mine, but the farther I walk, the more she stirs. When I reach the mudroom, her eyes flutter open, and she looks around, disoriented.

"Did I fall asleep?" she whispers.

Grinning, I nod. "You did. You and my dad." I wink. "Only one of you snored."

Her eyes widen, and I chuckle.

"Don't worry, Fireball. It was my dad."

Now that she's awake, I gently set her down on the bench next to the door and grab her shoes, smiling when I see she wore the deck boots I got her. One by one, I pull them slowly onto her feet, feeling my heartbeat pick up when I graze her leg on accident.

I stand up and pull on my own boots before tugging on my sweatshirt. When I grab her coat from the rack, her hand takes mine.

"Thank you, Ridge."

"For what?" I practically rasp, staring into her hazel eyes.

"For letting me stay when you could have made me leave." Tears well in her eyes. "This is the first real Christmas I've ever been a part of. And even though I didn't really deserve to be here, I'm so glad I was."

I sink down onto my heels and run the pad of my thumb against her soft cheek. She's not hiding behind a tough-girl act right now. She's letting me see her, down to her core, on what is probably the worst day of the year for her.

"I was happy to have you here, Fireball," I whisper, my heart breaking inside of my chest when a lone tear rolls down her face. "Merry Christmas."

"Merry Christmas." She smiles sadly.

I'm so fucking conflicted on what to do right now. Because even though I hate the thought of her being alone tonight, I don't want to complicate shit between us even more before she goes home. Especially if she doesn't want me to.

"Well, I guess I'll get you home," I say, halfway hoping she'll tell me she wants to stay with me.

"That would be great," she says.

I try to hide the disappointment on my face as I slowly push myself to stand and take her hand, helping her up along with me.

Sometimes, I think bad things happen for a good reason. Like the universe knows that in order to make shit go good, some things have to go south. And I believe it more than ever because, right now, Stella and I just found out that a tree had come down on the roof of the Jacobs' house while she was at my parents' house.

It may suck for them because this is their house and it's pretty damn nice—or was—but for me, it means Stella needs a place to stay because the roof now has a hole in it.

Bad for them. Good for me.

Even though she drives me fucking insane sometimes and I'm not sure I can fully trust the girl, I also can't shake the feeling that I need a little more time with her before she leaves. Just one more night to get her the hell out of my system.

I follow her through the house, holding my phone out, using it as a flashlight, as she gathers her stuff. She's frazzled—I don't know how she wouldn't be after the past few days' events. First, she got stuck in Maine, then had to drive home with me and Riley through a goddamn blizzard, and now, she has to rush through this house to collect her shit while the wind blows through.

She drags a hand over the top of her hair, looking around as her brows knit together with concern.

"Hey," I say, putting a hand on her shoulder. "We can come back tomorrow to make sure you didn't miss anything. It'll be light out and easier to see." I give her shoulder a slight rub with my hand in attempt to settle her. "Let's get out of here though, in case another tree comes down."

Sighing, she turns toward me. "Okay," she whispers.

I take her hand in mine and lead us back outside. The snow has finally stopped for the first time since yesterday morning, but the wind is still whipping around, blowing snow everywhere and making it impossible to see.

Heading for my truck, I go to the passenger side and feel around until my hand is on the door and pull it open. I help her get situated and close her in the warmth before throwing her bag into the back seat and jogging around to the driver's side.

Putting the truck in drive, I don't take off just yet, glancing over at her. Her hazel eyes are wide, and her face is pale.

"Hey," I say softly, putting my hand on hers. "You okay?"

Her eyes fly to my hand before slowly lifting to mine, and she nods weakly. "Yeah." She bobs her head up and down and gives me a tiny smile. "I am now. Thank you, Ridge. You just keep saving me." She swallows anxiously. "Are you sure it's okay I stay with you?"

"It'll cost you," I drawl, but when her eyes widen, I chuckle and lift my hand to her chin, brushing it. "Relax, Fireball. I'm only jokin.'"

But as I drop my hand from her face and turn my attention toward the road, I shift around in my seat as my cock swells. Because it doesn't matter that I fucked my hand in the shower this morning. My dick is already hardening when I think about being alone with her for an entire night.

Chapter 18

Stella

WE GET TO RIDGE'S HOUSE TO FIND THAT HE'S LOST POWER too. And his generator isn't working either. So, here he is in front of me, stoking the fire in the living room, while I bring pillows and blankets in from the closet he pointed me to so that we can sleep near the warmth tonight.

On the plush rug, I position the pillows and blankets far enough away from the fire so that we won't be charred to death, but close enough that we won't freeze into human Popsicles either. I spread our pillows out so that he doesn't think I'm assuming we're going to snuggle, even though my mind keeps wandering to doing that and much more. After all, it's Christmas. And we've already been together before, so what would be the harm in being together again?

"That should burn for a while," he says, setting the fire poker down and taking a few steps back to where I'm kneeling on the makeshift bed. "I can tell you, I've had this house for four years and never once used that fireplace."

"At least it's festive, right?" I smile. "Hopefully, you've been watering your beautiful tree. Otherwise, it might get a little toasty."

"And what a shame that would be," he drawls, amused. "And just so you know, I have been watering it. For your information, I've been watering the fuckin' thing twice a day. Pain in my ass it is." His tone is grumpy, and I can't help but giggle.

When he plops down beside me, his hand brushes mine, and I can't fight the shiver that runs down my spine. No one has ever had this sort of effect on me, and I don't know why he, out of all people, does. But I can't fight it, and I'm not even sure I want to. Especially not right now, when we're here all alone for Christmas.

"So ... you're leaving the day after tomorrow?" He keeps his eyes on the fire, not looking my way. "Right?"

"Yeah, that's the plan." My voice comes off much squeakier than I've ever heard it before. I'm not the girl who has a mousy voice when I'm around a man. And yet he makes me nervous. So, here I am, Squeaky McSqueakster. "As long as no more storms hit, I suppose."

"Last I looked, it should be clear for the next few weeks." He sounds so far away, despite being right in front of me. "I can take you to the airport. If you want."

My heart squeezes from his sweetness, but also aches because I know this time, my flight is going to take off, and we won't be on bad terms. And that will make it harder when I walk away.

"You don't have to do that," I say, shaking my head. "I feel like I've already inconvenienced you enough as it is."

"I promise you, Fireball, I don't mind," he mumbles. "Inconvenience me anytime you want. You're keeping my life interesting."

I can't stop blushing, and with his back still to me, I wave my hand in front of my cheeks to try to cool myself down. There's something about Ridge Adams's gentle side that turns me into a schoolgirl with her first crush, and I forget how to talk altogether.

I don't even have the chance to gather my bearings and answer before he's turning toward me. The flame from the fire dances across his cheeks, lighting up the sad expression on his face.

"Hey, Stella?" he murmurs, his shoulders sagging.

"Yeah?"

"I'm sorry you've never had a Christmas before today," he whispers, and even though his voice is still the same deep tone it always is, it's soft and comforting. "I wish I could have made your first one a little better than it was."

There it is. The sweet, thoughtful man that is inside, beneath the rough outer layer and the person he is when he's trying to be tough. We sit on the floor as the fire crackles with life. My throat becomes dry, and I shake my head, reaching for his hand and putting mine on top of it.

This man and his family have made me feel something inside my heart that I've never once felt on this particular day. Joy. And even though I'm not a part of their family, I kind of felt like ... I was today. I could leave it at this and tell him I'm tired. I could go to sleep, and tomorrow, maybe whatever this feeling is inside my chest would subside.

"It was great actually." I pause, my eyes boring into his, then sinking down to his lips before going back to his eyes. "If you have any DVDs, we can watch a Christmas movie or something on my dinosaur laptop, if you want?"

"That sounds good." He swallows, and the light from the fire illuminates his Adam's apple as it bobs. "I don't have a huge selection of DVDs, but I have a handful. You can pick."

That earns him a tiny smirk and a brow lift. "My pick, huh?" I muse. "Even a chick flick?"

"I love a good chick flick, babe." He shrugs softly. "Whatever you're feeling, that's what we'll watch."

The conversation we had about his parents flashes through my mind—about them staying in and watching whatever Katherine wanted to watch for a movie—and I can't stop myself from smiling. I had this man pinned wrong. He isn't a heartless dick. In fact, he's the opposite.

"A Christmas one actually sounds nice," I whisper. "Got any of those?"

A grin takes over his lips before he starts laughing. "Well, I do have one Christmas movie on DVD." Taking his phone out of his pocket to use the flashlight, he gets up and walks toward the entertainment center. Reaching inside, he pulls out something. And when I see it, I frown.

"*The Grinch*?" rushes from my lips. "You own the movie *The Grinch*?"

"Riley got it for me a few years back to be funny." He looks down at it. "I haven't watched the actual movie though since I was a kid." His eyes glimmer with amusement as he holds it up, waving it slightly. "Kinda fitting though … don't you think?"

"Oh, and what's that supposed to mean?" I roll my eyes toward the ceiling, shaking my head. "Are you trying to hint that I'm the Grinch, Outlaw?"

"Maybe we both are?" He shrugs. "But, yeah, Fireball, mostly you."

I stare at him, pretending to be in disbelief for a beat before I snatch the case from his hand and crouch down toward my laptop.

"I'll get this all started, and you can make the hot chocolate since you have a gas stove." I can hardly believe what's coming out of my mouth. Christmas is a holiday I barely acknowledge, and yet here I am, dragging it into the late-night hours. "And before you say you don't have any, there's a box in the bag I put on the counter. I had it at the rental house."

"All right, all right," he says with a grin, holding his hands up. "You got it. I think I may even have whipped cream to put on top."

The flirty way he says the last part of the sentence makes my heart skip a beat. And even if he didn't mean anything by it ... suddenly, I'm imagining Ridge with a can of whipped cream.

Naked.

Ridge

Stella only made it about twenty minutes into the movie before she fell asleep again. And things were fine, really.

Until she rolls onto her side, scooches her back into me, and presses her ass against my cock.

Even with the fucking movie playing and me telling myself over and over not to get hard, I can't help myself. And now, seconds later, my dick is hardening, pressing into her.

I shift, slowly rolling onto my back, knowing that I need to get up. Right now, I need to walk around and essentially ... walk off my boner, but just as I start to push myself to stand, her hand touches my wrist.

"Ridge?" she says sleepily, stopping me from actually getting up. "Where are you going?"

I look from her to my hard dick and back again. "Was just going to stretch, Fireball," I lie. My dick is already stretching.

And the longer she stays this close to me, the more he fucking grows. *Get it together, buddy.*

She sits up slightly, the fire still rolling and lighting her in the prettiest glow. She reaches for her laptop and closes it.

"Well, fuck you, Mr. Grinch," I tease her. "Didn't want to watch the part where his heart grows a bunch of sizes?"

With a shy shake of her head, she reaches for me and grips my shirt lightly. "Where were you really going, Outlaw?"

I swallow, knowing I can't lie to her. She'll see right through it.

"I was hoping a walk around the house would make my dick calm down." I shrug. "Having you this close excites me a bit." I look down. "Or … a lot."

I don't know what the fuck she's going to say. She could tell me to get away from her, that she's not interested and the one night we spent together was a mistake she'll long regret. With this woman, I never know what she's going to do.

But instead, she grips my shirt tighter.

"Show me," she whispers. "Show me what happens when I'm close to you."

"Stella …" I say nervously, not sure if she even knows what she wants. "It's Christmas. You're confused, and I don't want to take advan—"

My cock swells even harder, and my chin tilts up as I fight myself on all the reasons why I should just leave her alone and not make things even more complicated.

"Feel for yourself, Fireball," I murmur, moving onto to my side and letting my cock nudge into her leg. "One graze against your ass, and that's how hard I am."

She drops her hold on my shirt but slides her hand downward, pulling the fabric up so that her palm skims my stomach. The lower her hand moves, the harder my cock gets, and when she finally brushes her hand against my dick through my sweatpants, I groan.

"Is this my Christmas present?" she breathes out.

"If that's what you want, Stella … it's all yours."

"It's what I want," she whispers, running her palm over the bulge again. "Is it ready to be unwrapped?"

"Yes." I swallow, feeling my cock twitch. "Fuck. Yes. It is."

She looks to my right, and something catches her eye, but when she leans forward to grab whatever it is on the floor, I'm shook when she reveals a long piece of red ribbon. Because I don't know what she plans to do with that, but I hope she's about to tie me up.

Leaving the ribbon beside us, she reaches for the hem of my shirt. I let her peel it off before she climbs over me and hooks her fingers in the waistband of my sweatpants. Gradually, she pulls them, along with my briefs, down the length of my body, pushing them off before she crawls over me again.

Grabbing the ribbon, she holds it in front of me. "Hands behind your back, Outlaw. I'm going to be in control now."

The words leave her lips, and it takes me a few seconds to even fucking process them. But when I do, my hands are instantly behind my back, ready to be tied up. Because fuck if that's not the hottest thing I've ever heard before.

"And I want to fuck you bare. I have an IUD and was tested recently," she whispers, eyes looking into mine. "What about you?"

"Yes," I say quickly. "I've always been safe, and I get tested regularly. I promise."

Without another word, she crawls beside me, carefully wrapping the ribbon around my wrists and fastening it tightly. I watch her, so fucking turned on by whatever version of her this is right now.

Once she's done, she stands up, slowly stripping down in front of me. Her sexy silhouette is lit up by the glow from the fire. She unclasps her bra, letting it fall off her shoulders and onto the floor, leaving her perfect tits bare for me to admire.

"Fuck, you're so hot," I utter, staring up at a fucking wonder of the world. "Get your ass down here and ride me."

The last article of clothing is her panties, and soon, she's hooking her fingers under the band and pulling them down her legs. But instead of kicking them onto the floor, she balls them in her hand and steps one foot over me, giving me a perfect shot of her pussy.

Lifting one foot, she pushes it into my chest and tsks me. "I told you I was going to take control, and here you are, bossing me around, big guy," she coos. Each word is deliberate, like she knows exactly what she's doing. "Just for that, I think I need something to keep you quiet." She rolls the panties in her fingers, smirking down at me. "Open up, Outlaw. It's time to be a good boy and show me how quiet you can be while I ride your dick."

Lowering herself down, she brings the panties to my mouth. "Open," she says sharply.

And of course, I fucking open because when a sexy-as-hell redhead is naked in front of you, telling you to open your mouth so she can stuff her panties in it … you don't fucking hesitate.

Unhurriedly, she stuffs them in, letting some of the material hang from my lips before she cups my neck with both hands. "Such a good boy for me."

My cock is so swollen that I feel like I may go crazy if I don't fucking touch her soon. She's so close, and yet I can't be inside of her. Thank fuck she puts me out of my misery and begins to lower herself down.

When she sinks down to her knees, my cock nudges against her heat, and her eyes stay locked on mine. There's an animal inside of her—one I've never seen before—and her panties quiet a growl that so badly wants to tear from my throat.

Inch by inch, she dips herself lower. A small hiss slips from her lips, and she sucks in a breath through her teeth.

We spent the night making each other come, sure. But I've never actually fucked her before. And this isn't exactly what I had in mind for the first time I did. Not like I'm complaining though.

"You're so big," she practically whines.

Her nipples harden. I'm desperate to put my lips on them, but I can't. And I wish I could palm her tits with my hands, but I can't do that either. So, instead, I just enjoy the show.

Having my mouth stuffed with fabric and my heart beating a million miles an hour make it incredibly hard to breathe. But when she finally takes my entire dick deep inside of her and begins to ride ... fuck breathing. I'll die with a mouthful of panties with a fucking smile on my lips.

I'm completely at her mercy right now. Whether or not we both come is up to her. Yet something tells me my dick isn't going to last long because of how hot she is right now. Not just the way she looks, but how confident she is. Demanding what she wants and then taking it? Fucking sexy as hell.

"I bet you're so desperate to touch me right now, aren't you?" she breathes out, rocking slightly.

I nod sharply, though as much as I want to touch her, I like feeling like I'm her fucktoy right now, even though that's screwed up, I'm sure.

Her hands work their way up her own body, sliding up her sides to her breasts until she's cupping them. The sight of her playing with her tits while she rides my cock is too much, and I grunt hastily against the fabric.

Stella continues to palm her tits before she squeezes her nipples, riding me harder and faster, but through her pleasure, there's something else in her eyes too.

Frustration.

Her movements stop, and she pulls the panties from my mouth before shoving her tit against my lips. "Be quiet while you suck on my nipple, Ridge. Otherwise, I'll have to put the panties back in." She barely gets the last word out because my tongue is circling her nipple, and she cries out in pleasure, slamming her pussy down onto my dick once more.

I move my mouth over her tits, licking, biting, and kissing each one before shaking my head back and forth between them. And as I move to her right, dragging her nipple between my teeth and flicking my tongue back and forth, her hips rock faster as she grips my shoulders tightly.

I'm already a goner, but when her arm snakes around my body, and she cups my balls before massaging them in her fingers, there's absolutely no way to save me.

"Ridge …" She leans forward, pressing her forehead to mine. "Come with me … please."

With her hand still playing with my balls and my cock buried deep inside of her, I fight to keep my eyes open and my vision clear as cum shoots from my cock and straight inside of her while her orgasm rips through her, making her scream out while her pussy convulses around me.

I've never come inside anyone my entire life. I've always worn a condom. I hardly know this woman, and she hardly knows me, yet here I am, filling her full and loving every second of it.

My body trembles just as her rocking stops, and she dips her forehead back to mine and huffs out a shaky breath.

I'm not sure what to even say right now. I don't know if she's going to scurry away like she did last time or maybe look panicked. Instead, she grins.

"Well, that was fun. But maybe we should finish *The Grinch*," she murmurs playfully. "I mean, if his heart really does grow a bunch of sizes, I need to see this."

"You haven't seen it before?" I ask, instantly wishing I hadn't said anything because she'll probably feel bad now. I don't know any kid who hasn't seen *The Grinch* because it's a classic. But then again, it seems as though her childhood wasn't exactly warm. I mean, the girl had never even had a proper Christmas until today.

"Well, I have as of tonight." She giggles before she unwraps her body from mine. "By the end of it, I'll know who's more of a Grinch. You or me."

"Pfft ..." I snort. "I've got a spoiler for you, Fireball. It's you."

"We'll just see about that," she sasses, grabbing her laptop and placing it in front of us again. "After all, your brother got *you* the movie for Christmas."

Snuggling against me, she seems to genuinely relax as we lie on the living room floor.

And I enjoy every fucking second of it.

Chapter 19

Ridge

THE MOVIE HAS BEEN OVER FOR A WHILE NOW, AND YET WE LIE here, wide awake and still naked.

"How bad is it going to be for you?" I ask her while she lies beside me, so close that her head is using my chest as a pillow. I'm not complaining though. This may be the best Christmas I've ever had, and that's no joke. "When you get back to the city and break it to your boss that this place is a dead end for him, how mad will he be?"

She's silent—lost in her own thoughts, I guess—while the fire crackles beside us. At first, when we got here earlier, I was pissed that my generator wasn't working because it'd never given me trouble, and of course, it had to start tonight, when she was going to be staying here. But after what we just did on the floor and how hot she looked in the light of the fire while I fucked her from behind as my balls slapped her ass in the damn near-silent house? I'll take a power outage any day if it means this is what comes of it.

"Honestly?" She lets out a long sigh, keeping her head to my flesh. "I think I'm for sure going to lose my job. But to tell you the truth, if I could, I'd just quit anyway." She breathes out a quiet, almost-sad laugh. "Probably would have quit a long time ago, when they made Victor my boss with literally no training."

I make sure to think before I speak right now. Stella can be sweet, but she also has a fire that's always burning inside of her. Feistiness in a woman has never drawn me in—before her. Now, I love watching that fire ignite. But I also know that she's skittish, and I don't want to say anything that she may take the wrong way or offend her. While fishing and the wharf are my legacy, she has her own, I'm sure. And even though her boss sounds like a prick, that's her career. It means something to her.

"Why can't you quit?" I ask, pausing because I know I need to expand what I just said. "I don't mean that to sound judgmental. I just mean, you said you would if you could. So, I guess I'm wondering, if it's okay that I ask, what's keeping you there? What are your reasons?"

I'm met with more silence, which I'll admit I expected. She's guarded; that's been clear to see since our day at the tree farm.

"I don't come from a loving family like the one you have, Ridge. And truthfully, even though I don't love my job, it's a job that pays well enough for me to have a beautiful apartment and everything else I need. But most of all, it makes me feel secure in life." She breathes in sharply. "There was a time when I didn't even have a roof over my head. And when I did have a roof over my head, the people I was living with were so awful that I would have rather been homeless."

Even though I can't see her face, she suddenly nuzzles it into my side, like she needs to hide from me.

"I've worked really hard to get to a place in my life where I feel safe, and I just … the thought of losing that is actually debilitating for me."

There's so much I don't know about this woman, but I know I can't spring twenty questions on her right now, even if that's what I want to do. I want to know everything about her, not just these small tiny pieces. But little by little, I'm figuring out why she is the way that she is.

Sharp yet soft at times. And sassy, though sometimes bashful too.

"And all of that … is that why you've never celebrated Christmas?" My chest hurts as I ease out the question. "And why you didn't want to go to the tree farm?"

A sad laugh slips from her lips. "My parents sucked, and once I was taken from them and put into foster care when I was ten, they didn't even bother to try to get clean and get me back. Instead, they just kept on doing drugs, and eventually, they got something that was laced, and they both overdosed."

The words come out almost robotic, and I have no idea how I know this, but I'm somehow sure that she's never said these words out loud before. She's too tough for that, and I think that in her mind, if she runs from her past, it can't bother her. So, she puts on her tough armor, and she runs.

"My whole life, I've watched everyone around me—in school and at jobs—love Christmas because of who they got to spend it with." She runs her palm against my chest. "This was the first Christmas where I got to be a part of something like that. And I know that sounds odd and probably creepy because, well, it's your family and all, and I'm just a stranger. But I was there, and I felt the love you have for each other and the adoration your mom has for a holiday that she bases around her family." She quickly buries her face harder against me. "You must think I'm—"

Quickly, I sit up, dragging her up with me, though she only buries her face against my shoulder now. "Stella, look at me," I say, trying to cup her cheeks and force her head upward. "Please, beautiful, just look at me."

"I'm so embarrassed," she whispers, and I hardly hear her. "Here you all were, giving me a pity invite to Christmas, not even knowing it was the first holiday I'd ever been a part of."

Instead of forcing her to look at me, now, I bury my face against her hair and kiss the top of her head over and over again. "You're embarrassed because you enjoyed being with my family today?" I utter. "Well, guess what? Having you at Christmas made it feel like a real holiday for me. Having you there made it the best one I'd had in a long damn time."

Forever actually. But I don't want to scare you away.

Not right away, but slowly, she lifts her head up. Her eyes are wet, and her lips are pouty. "You're just trying to make me feel better."

"No, I'm not," I say, shaking my head. "My mom loves Christmas. And because of that, I always go and do all the shit she asks of me. But every year, I watch the clock, excited for it to be over so I can come the hell home." I cup her cheeks, kissing her forehead. "But this year, I loved having you there so much that we ended up being the last ones to leave." I know that what I'm about to say is going to sound insane, but I'm going to say it anyway. "Having you there, around my family? It felt right, Stella."

I don't know who this version of me is. Even the few girlfriends that I've had never got this much emotion out of me, and they were certainly never at Christmas, and I wouldn't have wanted them to be either. What's crazy is, I spent more time with them than I have with Stella, but I feel like I somehow know her more, even though I hardly know her at all. And this feeling inside my chest every single time we come together, I don't get it either. Sex is sex, but with her … that's not true. I feel her everywhere when we're together.

But aside from my family, I've never loved anyone. And I can't love her; it's too soon for that.

It *has* to be. It hasn't even been two full weeks.

She sniffles, smiling, though more tears fall. "I know that your family is probably wary of me, and they have every right to be—so do you. But thank you for letting me be a part of your world for the day." Her lips tremble. "Your family and this place, Holiday Harbor, have changed me. I can't even explain it, but it's true."

Her head dips forward, and her lips press to mine. Instantly, my cock begins to harden yet again. Her kiss intensifies and I drag my hand down her face, cupping her neck gently.

"Ride me again, Stella," I growl into her mouth. "I need to feel that pussy squeeze my cock once more before Christmas is over."

Moving around, she swings her leg over my thighs and straddles me before dropping the blanket down, exposing her perfect tits in the light of the fire, and my dick grows against her slit, needing to be inside of her.

"Look at you, hard again already," she says, dipping her lips to my ear. "Fill me up once more, Outlaw. It's Christmas, and for my gift, all I want is to be full of you."

I tremble from her words before I slide my palms down her body. I lift her just enough so that her pussy is hovering over my aching cock, but before I even get the chance to lower her slowly, she sits down on it, filling herself so full of my dick, taking me so deep that a hiss slips from her lips.

Keeping myself upright, I move us both backward until my back is against the couch. And with her arms around my neck and her face just inches from mine, she fucks me, thrusting her hips, making my brain fucking mad.

She slides up and down on my length, taking me deeper each time she lowers herself. Her eyes are locked on mine, and a sheer layer of sweat beads on her beautiful, porcelain-like skin. She doesn't say a word, but she doesn't have to because the dazed-off expression in her eyes tells me everything while she continues to ride my cock.

I love the look in her eyes when she's losing herself in me.

"That's it, baby," I grunt.

When she lifts herself again, I bury my face between her tits before working my way to each one and dragging my tongue over the nipple and sucking. A loud moan rolls from her lips, and she slams her pussy down onto my length harder.

"Take what you need. Show me how much of a slut you can be when it comes to my cock."

"Ridge," she moans out, rubbing herself against me when she sits down on it this time, rocking ever so slightly.

Raking my fingernails down her back, I look up at her and bite down on her neck. "Do you think you can make my dick come again?" I growl against her flesh.

"Yes," she hisses with her chin angled toward the ceiling when I fist her hair and give it a yank. "I'm going to make you come inside of my pussy."

"Yeah?" I barely choke out, releasing my hold on her hair and moving my hands to her tits. With one on each, I cup them while she starts riding me again. "Come on, slutty girl. Don't stop riding my dick until my cum is leaking from your pussy and dripping down my thighs."

Her nails dig into my shoulders, and she thrusts her hips back and forth as her mouth hangs open while she's gasping for air. The harder her nails prod into my flesh, the more my balls start to tingle.

Her pussy tightens, squeezing my dick greedily just as she moans loudly.

"Cover my dick while I fill up that sweet, tight pussy," I grunt just as she begins to pulsate around me.

Her thrusts become inconsistent, and cum explodes from the tip of my cock as I blow my load inside of her, claiming her as mine in my own fucked-up way.

Her body collapses against mine as her rocking gets slower and slower, and I tremble against her, damn near feeling like I may black out.

Even after our orgasms are over, she stays against me, holding on to me tightly. And I realize that I don't know if there will ever be a time I'm with her when I don't want her again after.

I keep telling myself one more time is all I need, but the truth is, I know that's bullshit. Because it'll never be enough.

Unfortunately, it has to be because, in two days, she'll be gone forever.

Chapter 20

Stella

AFTER BRUSHING MY TEETH, COMBING MY HAIR OUT, AND washing my face, I look at myself in the mirror. It's the day after Christmas, and for the first time in I don't even know how many years, I'm not hungover from drinking alone while trying to numb the sadness from the night before. Instead, Ridge and I spent the entire night naked, in front of the fireplace, giving each other orgasm after orgasm—always coming together too.

To be honest, I'm a little sad that the power is back on because I had such a good time in the dark. There was just something about the fire and us being the only source of keeping each other warm that was so sexy and intimate. But there's an aching in my gut, and I know it's because tomorrow, I'm flying back to the city.

Walking out of the bathroom, I head into the kitchen to find Ridge sitting on a barstool, drinking his coffee with a second cup beside him. Steam flows from the top, and I smile as I walk around the island and plop down beside him.

"Happy to have the power back?" I say, leaning toward him and pressing my shoulder to his.

"Kinda." He cranes his neck to look down at me and smirks. "Though I gotta say, that whole … sex all night long by the fire was pretty hot." He raises his brows up and down. "I didn't know my dick was capable of coming that many times or staying hard that long." He winks. "Kinda think I have a superpower."

I roll my eyes but laugh. "Or maybe it's me with the superpower for making you capable of doing that." I shrug. "Ever think about that?"

"Oh, is that it?" he drawls, tickling my side. Or attempting to. "Are you seriously not ticklish?"

"Nope," I say flatly. "Not even a little."

"That's … kind of creepy," he utters. "So, you're leaving tomorrow. Aside from all the snow, it's fairly warm out today, so I figured I could show you a few things in the area before you have to go back to the big city and forget all about this place." He nudges me playfully. "Some … local treasures, I guess you could say."

"That sounds perfect," I answer, trying not to think about what it's going to be like to leave here tomorrow. "What's first on your list?"

"You'll see," he says cryptically before he slides from the stool, tugging me up with him. "Get your ass ready, woman. Time is ticking!"

As I rush toward his room to get ready for the day, I force myself to ignore the ache in my chest. I need to enjoy what time I have left with a man, who, not many days ago, I couldn't stand. And now? All I want to do is have more time with him.

Maybe it's a good thing I have to leave Holiday Harbor tomorrow. Any more time spent here, and I'd fall for this fisherman. And Lord knows that it would never work between us.

Ridge

I tell myself that I'm just showing her around the town to be nice and to give her the full Maine experience, but the truth is, I think a part of me is hoping she'll love it so much that she won't want to leave. I don't know why anyone who visits here would want to leave. It's beautiful. And peaceful. But I suppose the things I love about my home state might be things that she doesn't love. That's why she loves the city, which is just another reason it could never work between us.

Still, I don't know how tomorrow is going to go when I drop her off at the airport. I know that it'll be hard as hell to say goodbye to her. But will she be sad? Or maybe secretly happy to get back to her life? I don't fucking know. All I know is, I like having her here. I'm not ready for her to go.

Maybe it was meant to be a short-lived fling, but that's not how I see it anymore.

We walk along our first stop, which is a beach that sits on my cousin's land. It's the next town over from mine, but where most of our oceanfront is rocky, his has an actual sand beach. But the beach isn't the best part; it's the old shipwreck that's on the tiny island in front of it.

"That is so cool," Stella whispers, staring out at the water. "When did that happen?"

"Back about thirty years ago or so. It was a rough night, and the ship broke free from its mooring and went up on its side out there." I wave toward it. "They decided to keep it there for history reasons because the boat belonged to a rich guy who owned a big chunk of the town."

She looks from me and back to the shipwreck before, suddenly, she laughs. "That story isn't nearly as cool as I thought it was going to be." She tilts her head to the side. "Here I thought, you were going to tell me that it was a pirate ship or something off the wall."

"Well, fuck you then," I deadpan. "I'm sorry; let me make something up. It was people looking for treasure two hundred years ago. Pirates saw them and realized they were looking for the same thing, and they decided to fire at them, making the ship capsize and eventually wash up." I shrug my shoulders. "Not a single survivor, and they say, sometimes, their bones still wash up on these shores."

She stares at me. Then, slowly, her lips turn up, and she pats my arm. "All right, *that* right there was the story I was looking for. Thank you. Now, I'm satisfied, and anyone who asks me about the shipwreck in Maine, I'm sharing that story, not the lame-ass first one."

"Yeah, okay," I murmur, poking her side. "Speaking of satisfied, you seemed satisfied last night." I pause. "Many times."

"Oh, pfft. Get over yourself." She narrows her eyes, but when I hold her gaze, she rolls them. "Fine." She throws her head back, holding her arms out. "I was highly satisfied. Happy now?"

"I will be if we can repeat it again tonight." I flash her a small grin. "And maybe in the morning before your flight leaves too. After all, I need to fill you so full that I'll be with you after you're gone."

Amused, she looks down before grabbing a few flat rocks and holding them up. "If you can skip a single rock six times, you've got yourself a deal." She passes me two of them. "I'll give you two tries."

"And if I can't do it?" I ask, knowing damn well I can do more than six skips, but wanting to play along with her little game.

"Well, I guess you'll have to satisfy yourself," she coos.

"That's fine; I've been doing that in the shower every day since you got here." I shrug. "Only the first few times, I had to picture a fantasy. And now, well, I've fucked you so many different ways that I have all kinds of material up here to use when I stroke my dick." I point to my head.

Her eyes widen as her mouth hangs open. "You're gross!" She attempts to pretend to be offended before waving toward the water. "Go on, big guy. Show me what you got. Let's determine if you'll get your spank-bank version of me or the real thing."

I do my best to seem unsure of myself, not wanting to lead on that I'm stupidly competitive. Growing up, I was always the rock-skipping champ against my brothers. Maybe it's from having siblings or playing sports throughout my high school days. Either way, I can't stand to lose, so I try to make it a point to never do that.

Walking to the edge of the beach, I turn to the side, curve my wrist just right, and skim the rock against the water. I stand there and watch circle after circle appear at the top of the water.

"Eight?" she yells. "Eight on the first try? I feel hustled." She shakes her head. "That doesn't count. That was a practice one."

"You never asked if I was good at it." I shrug, taunting her. "Care to make it ten skips?"

Her mouth hangs open, and she puts a hand on her hip. "Ten?" she gasps. "Fine. You know what? Ten it is!"

Taking the other rock into my hand, I get in my stance. But this time, instead of looking out at the water, I lock eyes with her. "I'm so nervous," I say sarcastically in a smart-ass tone. "So much on the line here."

Keeping my gaze on hers, I haul back and skip the rock. Her eyes dart from mine to the water, and she gulps again. Her lips move as she counts the skips.

"Who are you, Nathan Scott? Trying to lock eyes while taking an important shot?" she barks out. "Twelve. You freaking got twelve."

"I have no idea who Nathan Scott is, but if you tell me how many rocks he skipped, I'll make sure I put him to shame," I say truthfully. "Was it some crazy number like thirty though? If so, I may need more practice rocks."

"He's from the television series, *One Tree Hill*, you moron," she says, shaking her head. "Anyway, you got twelve. Now you can stop showing off."

"Oh good. I thought he was my competition or something," I admit. "And first, you said six. And then ten. Since I got twelve, I think I should get a little something extra."

"Oh, yeah?" She folds her arms over her chest, narrowing her eyes, but it's clear as day she's fucking excited. "Like what?"

I tap my chin. "Like … a blow job in the truck. Or maybe I can eat your ass."

I watch her shiver, and I know it's not from the cold air. She's a filthy girl, and I wish she could stay longer so I could see just how fucking dirty she likes to get.

"What do you say, Fireball?" I prod, stepping closer to her and putting my arms around her waist. "You're leaving tomorrow, and I still haven't gotten my fix."

I say it like we're both treating this whole thing like it's light and a joke, but something about what I just said actually fucking hurts too. There's an elephant in the room. One that needs to be addressed. But I guess we're both too proud to say it out loud and ask where the fuck we go from here.

Her expression grows somber, and she gazes up at me.

"It wouldn't have mattered if you hadn't gotten any skips. I still would have been in your bed—or on the living room floor—tonight."

Standing on her tippy-toes, she waits for me to bend down and kiss her. I don't keep her waiting long before pressing my lips to hers. And when I'm done, she slides her hands against my sides.

"Next destination?" she whispers.

"Next destination," I say back. Excited to show her so many places, but also dreading each one because it's that much closer to her leaving.

I take her hand in mine as we walk back toward where my truck is parked along the road. I'm glad she has the boots on that I got her because even though the snow didn't amount to much once it got blown

around in the wind, there are still some drifts, and since it's above freezing today, everything is melting, making it a wet mess.

Exactly like I hope she is for me tonight.

As we reach my truck and I go to open the door, a voice stops me.

"Just on a romantic walk, coz?" the deep voice calls out, and I grin
when I see my cousin walking toward us.

"Holy shit," Stella whispers. "That's Knox Carter. As in … retired
NFL player Knox Carter." She looks up at me, eyes wide. "*He's* your
cousin?"

"He is, but don't get too excited. He's married, and I'm suddenly a
jealous man," I murmur playfully just before he reaches us.

"Yeah, now my big-shot cousin is here to show me up!" I grin at him.
"How're Sloane and the kids?"

"They're good," he says proudly. "They're up at the house, taking
down the Christmas tree. As much as Sloane loves to decorate—way too
fucking early, like *before Thanksgiving* early—that woman hardly lets the
last present be passed out before she starts putting shit away."

"That's better than my mother." I laugh. "She'll leave hers up well
after New Year's. Loves it." I chuckle again before I turn slightly toward
Stella. "Knox, this is Stella. Stella, this is my hotshot cousin—"

"Knox Carter," Stella says, cutting me off while she stares at him. "I
am a huge football fan, and though your time in the NFL was short, you
certainly made an impact."

I try not to laugh as she completely fangirls out on my cousin.
Everyone around town is used to him being out and about, but for her,
I'm sure it's insane to run into him like this, and I know she just made his
entire day. He gave up football a while back so that he could be there for
his kids while they grew up. I know he's always been more than happy
with his decision, but leaving had to have been hard for him too.

"Thank you, thank you," he drawls, flashing her a pleased grin before
he looks down at her boots. "My wife has those boots. Along with about
… five other colors."

She smiles at me. "Thanks. Ridge forced me to get them, and now I
think I also need, like, five more pairs." She laughs. "I'll admit, I can see
the appeal. Comfortable, warm, and cute."

We chat for a few minutes before he takes a step back.

"Well, I've gotta run to the store, but I saw you down here and just had to say hi." He shakes my hand again. "I hope you two had a good Christmas." He winks at Stella, and then his eyes dart between ours. "It's nice to see my cousin finally settling down."

We look nervously at each other, both cringing.

"Oh, we're not …" Stella says, but stops.

I don't bother trying to explain anything. Instead, I just hold my hand up and wave goodbye to him, and once he turns and is walking away, I pull her in for a hug.

"Next stop?"

Smiling up at me, she nods shyly. "Next stop."

Chapter 21

Stella

I CAN'T SEEM TO GET OUT OF THIS FUNK I'M IN, NO MATTER WHAT I DO. I tossed and turned all night, but whenever I looked over at Ridge, he seemed to be doing the same thing.

Today is the day when I leave Maine in the past and head back to my life in New York, not even knowing if a job will be there waiting for me, but I can't stay. I have responsibilities back home.

Besides, I've only known him for two weeks. It's insane of me to even consider staying longer for a man I hardly know. I'm just lost in a . . . Maine Christmas bubble. Where everything is like a spicy Hallmark movie. Once I'm home, I'll be pulled out of it, and I'll remember how much I love where I live, and I'll forget about Ridge. I'm sure of it.

It's early. So early that the sun isn't even up, and yet here I am, staring at the ceiling. I'm afraid to look over at him because if he's awake, that means we probably need to have a conversation. And right now, I'm not sure what good talking would do. Deep down, we both know what this is. It's a fling. And flings are meant to be uncomplicated and fun.

Unfortunately for me, Ridge must know that I'm lying here awake because when I feel the bed shift as he rolls to his side, I can sense his eyes on me.

"You know what I said about my favorite view of this place being from the water?" His voice isn't groggy like it should be for a time when we should be asleep. Instead, he sounds wide awake. Then again, he's used to getting up much earlier than this for work.

"Yeah, I remember." I don't roll onto my side to look at him. Instead, I keep my gaze upward. Looking into his eyes right now would break my heart.

We aren't strangers anymore. I've told him things about my life that I've never said to anyone else—aside from a therapist I had for a short time.

"Since your flight isn't till later … can I show you?" For a tough, rugged man, he speaks so softly right now, like he's walking on eggshells because he doesn't want to spook me. "If we hurry, we can catch the sunrise too."

Every intimate moment I spend with this man is only going to make it harder to walk away from him. But my entire adult life, I've been so fixated on controlling situations after feeling like I had no control at all for so long. Right now, I don't want to be anxious, thinking about the pain that's to come. I just want to continue to feel. So, rolling onto my side, I reach up and brush my palm against the stubble on his face.

"I would love that," I whisper.

And the look in his eyes only makes the pain radiate deeper through my chest. Because just like me, he's dreading tonight. I can see it.

So many sounds flood my ears, but each one is peaceful and projects a sort of calmness that I'd never be able to explain to my coworkers in the city.

The dull rumble of the boat's engine somehow seems like that of a lullaby. And the waves hitting against the sides of the boat, splashing softly as it cuts through the salty water, provide some sort of mystical, calming effect. Maybe some people would find the squawk of the seagulls off in the distance annoying, but as I take a deep breath of sea air, I feel a sense of home in a place that's the furthest thing from it.

It's dusk, and I stand beside Ridge as he keeps one hand on the wheel and the other on the space that looks sort of like a dashboard, but … on a boat. He's showing me a piece of himself. A piece that makes up such a big part of who he is, and I see him so clearly right now. More than ever before.

This place is enough for him. He's happy here, in Maine, doing what he loves. What a feeling that must be—to just know you're exactly where you belong and have been your whole life. I envy that kind of feeling. I've never had that, and I also don't know if I ever will.

"Wanna drive?" he asks, looking down at me. "We'll steam to the lighthouse. That's the best place to see the sunrise."

"Oh … I don't know," I say, chewing my lip. I do want to drive his boat. I've never driven any boat—ever. And his is gorgeous, but it's his livelihood. I don't want to make a mistake and hurt it. "That's okay. I don't want to hurt your boat or anything."

Unfazed, he lifts a brow. "Do you plan on running it into a ledge as payback for anything mean I said?"

"Well, no," I say quickly. "Of course not. I don't want to die." I cringe. "I'm actually a terrible swimmer. I'd never make it."

His eyebrows dip down thoughtfully before he grins. "Okay then, you're driving."

Taking a step back, he plants his hands on my waist and shifts my body in front of the ship's wheel. Nervously, I grip it, keeping it straight and trying to ignore his hands on my body because I have a damn boat to drive.

"Like this?" I whisper, painfully aware of his hands still.

"Yep," he says. "You're doing great, Fireball."

It may seem like no big deal, yet my heart races, and my skin prickles to life. I don't know if it's from having Ridge so close, driving a boat for the first time, or a combination of both. All I know is, I've been on a lot of dates, and none of them have ever come close to the one I'm on right now.

In the distance, I see the outline of the lighthouse as the sun begins to ascend. When I looked at the pictures of Maine before coming here, I knew it was going to be beautiful. What I didn't know was how much the beauty would impact me.

"Wow," I whisper as the light slowly hits the lighthouse.

I've seen plenty of calendars and screensavers, but nothing compares to this moment right now. I'm in a boat, watching the sun rise next to a gorgeous lighthouse.

I can't believe I didn't want to come to Maine when I first found out I had to.

"I think I take for granted that this is my office," Ridge says slowly, only half teasingly. "One hell of a view, huh?"

I don't know what it is, but tears threaten to spring in my eyes, and my throat grows hoarse with raw emotion as I swallow it down and nod. "Yeah. It sure is."

Once we get close enough to it, Ridge reaches around me and pulls a throttle that takes the boat out of gear. Walking to the back of the boat, he picks up a large anchor that is clearly heavy before he steps onto the side of the boat and carries it to the bow. I watch in awe, not knowing how someone could ever be this comfortable on the ocean. And despite the sunrise being at its peak, I can't take my eyes off him as he ties the rope to the very front of the boat and throws the anchor over. Once he's done, he walks back down the side of the boat, past the thing that swings—something that I'm pretty sure lifts his traps out of the water—and jumps back down next to me.

Though I try to fight myself from shivering, I fail, and of course, Ridge notices.

"Inside the wheelhouse is nice and warm," he says, pointing toward the door that leads into a closed-in area on the deck. "We can sit in there and watch the rest of the sunrise." He pauses. "Or . . . look at the cool color the sky is now that the sun has risen."

Laughing lightly, I shiver again and follow him through the door. Once he's closed it behind us, he plops down on the captain's chair with yet another ship's wheel in front of it before patting his lap.

"Come sit with me, city girl. Let's look at the sunrise together." He stops, shrugging playfully. "They say nothing beats a Maine sunrise. Maybe it'll convince you to stay here. Who knows?"

His words don't piss me off; they just make everything I've been trying to avoid feeling hit me all at once. The truth is, I love everything about Maine. And everything about this place is making me question the city.

But here's the catch that I keep going back to . . . is it Maine, or is it a certain guy in Maine? One I hardly know.

I am one of the most levelheaded people I know. I don't make rash decisions. I think about everything from every angle possible, and then I decide what comes next. But even considering staying here is insanity. I know it is. And yet the thought is secretly dancing in the back of my mind.

"What are you saying, Ridge?" I shrug, unable to enjoy the damn sky anymore because all I can think about is the stupid words he just said. "That you want me to stay here?"

He doesn't even know how to answer me, which only makes me more upset.

"Do you want me here for good, or do you just want me here a few more days for sex?" I blurt out, knowing I sound like a crazy person, but I can't seem to stop myself from spewing out more bullshit. "Is that all this is to you? Sex?"

He stands abruptly and takes a few large strides to me and glares down.

"What's it to you, Stella? Is it sex? Is it a distraction from the holidays? Is that what I am to you?"

"I don't—" I stop, bringing my hands to my face. "I don't know! Okay? Is that what you want to hear? I don't fucking know what this is anymore!"

"Well, do you want to stay?" He wastes no time barking out, "Or do you miss New York?"

I stare at him, my eyes dancing between his, and he throws his arms up.

"It's not a hard question, Stella! You either want to stay here longer, or you want to go home. Answer me!"

"Stay here?" I yell, dropping my hands. "Ridge, I hardly know you! And you're asking if I want to stay here?"

"You know me," he hisses through gritted teeth. "You know me better than any other woman ever has. I don't give a fuck that we met two weeks ago. I've never spent Christmas with a girl. Or made her coffee. No other woman has ever stepped foot on my boat besides my mother, and I sure as hell have never taken a date sightseeing."

"I don't even know your middle name, Ridge." I shake my head. "Or how old you are. I don't know who your last girlfriend was or if you've had your heart broken." I inhale. "I know nothing about you. And you don't know me either."

His chest heaves while he stares at me before, finally, he turns away. He's silent for a few moments. Eventually, he talks.

"My middle name is Mathew, after my dad. I'm twenty-eight. My birthday is in the spring. My last girlfriend, if you can call her that, her name was Natalie, but we dated only for two months, and then I broke up with her. I've never had my heart broken—until now." Turning to face me, he walks so that his body is inches from mine. "If you leave tomorrow, you're going to break my fucking heart, Stella."

"Ridge," I whimper. "Stop."

"No," he replies sharply. "I know that you've been through more pain than anyone should ever have to go through. I know that Christmas isn't easy, and yet you were the highlight of my family's get-together, just by being yourself. I know you put on a tough act, but inside, you're sweet." Reaching for my cheek, he brushes his fingers against my skin. "And I know you don't love your job, but you love the security of a steady paycheck and being able to afford a nice place to live. Because after years of having neither of those things, you aren't ready to give it up."

Tears blur my vision, and quickly, I look away from him. "I can't give up everything to move here with a guy I just met less than two weeks ago, Ridge. I won't."

"And I can't follow you to New York because my livelihood—my entire life—is here," he rasps. "Even if I wish I somehow could … New York … it's just not my scene."

Tears roll down my cheeks, and I sniffle. "So, it's decided then?" I croak. "This thing … you and I, it could never work."

"I guess not." His voice is gravelly now.

I stare up at him through tear-soaked lashes. He's not dressed in a suit or fancy shoes, like the men in the city are, but that makes him even handsomer. Right now, he stares down at me in his simple hoodie and baseball hat, making this moment hurt even more. Cupping my face, he brings his mouth to mine, and both of our eyes flutter shut as he kisses me deeply.

"Fuck me one last time, Ridge," I sob against his lips. "Please. I'm not ready to never feel you again."

He groans, "Stella, I'm going to fill your tight hole so fucking full that, just like I promised, I'll be with you long after you're gone."

"And what about you?" I whimper. "You'll just get to be free of me once I leave? Is that it?"

"I know for a fact that no woman will ever make my cock as hard as you do, baby." He slips his tongue into my mouth, and between our pants, I feel his erection poking against me. "All it takes is this fucking mouth being sassy, or one small touch, and my dick turns to steel."

"Take it out," I cry desperately. "I need your cock. I need you."

"You take it out," he rasps. "Do that one last thing for me."

Dipping my hands down, I reach between us and unbutton his jeans and push his briefs down. I don't take his jeans all the way off, but just enough to give me what I need.

When I put my thumb to the tip, pre-cum wets my skin, and I bring it up and drag my tongue across my finger. "I love the way you taste," I breathe out, loving the whimper that erupts from his throat.

Dropping to my knees, I stare up at him through tear-soaked eyes as I bring him into my mouth. I'm ready to make sure he never forgets how good my lips can make him feel. Or how hard my tongue can make him come.

And I'll never forget the look in his eyes when he stares at me with pure desperation. Because no man has ever looked at me quite like that before.

Until Ridge.

Ridge

"Fuck … baby. That's it," I grunt. "Your throat feels so good while I'm driving my dick down it."

I rock my hips against her, thrusting my cock further down her throat. I'm damn near close to choking her, but she takes me inch by inch, not even batting a fucking eyelash.

I'm really going to miss this fucking girl.

"Wish I could fill every fucking hole of yours," I choke out, using the armrest of the chair and her hair as leverage to rock myself deeper into her throat. "Leave a piece of me inside of every part of you so that you'd never be the same."

Wet lips and a soft, warm tongue work their way up and down my length as her big eyes stare up at me. I don't need to rock my hips or thrust her face harder against me because she's sucking my dick like she's on a mission to earn a mouthful of cum. And if she keeps it up, that's exactly what she's going to get.

I'm so close, but I'm also scared to death that the second I come, she's going to think this is over. She'll want to go back to shore and run away from me, and I can't let her do that. So, instead of filling her throat full, I decide to heave her up onto her feet.

Yanking her leggings down, I lift her and set her on the bulkhead in front of where my captain's chair is before I climb into it and look forward at her.

"Spread your legs, baby," I grunt, palming my cock. "I'm going to fuck my hand while I watch you play with that tight pussy."

Reluctantly, her hand slowly works its way down her abdomen, stopping between her legs. But still, she doesn't spread them apart. I give her another few seconds—until I'm too impatient. Then I lean forward, spreading them apart abruptly, and a hushed whimper leaves her lips.

"Be a good girl and show me how you're going to play with yourself when I'm not around."

I palm myself again, relaxing back and taking in the sight of her spread eagle in front of me. It doesn't matter that there's a beautiful lighthouse or morning sky behind her. All I see are her glazed-over eyes, her pretty pink pussy, and the gorgeous face of an angel.

"Only if you show me what you're going to do when I'm gone," she whispers breathily. "And tell me what it is you see in your head when you do it."

Reaching my hand out to her, I put my palm in front of her mouth. "Get my hand nice and wet, just like your pussy always is for me."

There's no hesitation; she drags her tongue along my palm before spitting on my skin, and I give her a small nod.

"Good girl. Well, first, I'll probably think about that look in your eyes whenever you need my cock," I start, and with my palm nice and soaked, I wrap it around my aching cock and begin to stroke. "Because you're a little slut for my cock, aren't you, baby?"

"Yes," she chokes out, circling the pad of two fingers over her clit before sinking a finger inside of herself. "I'll think about how your cock always looks so fucking hot that I can't help but drop to my knees and suck it."

"Yeah, you love sucking my dick, don't you, Stella?" I coo. "You love feeling me hit the back of your throat while you're choking for air."

"I do," she whines, fucking herself harder. "This just isn't the same as your dick, Ridge."

Flipping my hat backward, I lean forward and drive my face between her thighs, nudging her hand out of the way before I push my tongue inside of her with no warning. I continue to stroke my dick because I think it may explode if not. And with her head pressed against the front window, I eat her like she's the first piece of cake I've ever seen after being deprived of sweets my whole life.

Tipping my head back, I spit against her heat before using my fingers and shoving them inside of her. I sit back in my seat, but this time, I yank her along with me, making it so she's straddling me now.

"Wrap my cock up in that tight pussy, Fireball," I growl into her mouth. "Sink right down onto me and let me feel what I wish were mine."

Lifting her hips slightly, she lowers herself down. Between my spit and her being so fucking turned on, she's soaked, and she slides down my length, feeling like fucking heaven.

I wrap my arms around her, gripping her by her ass cheeks. "No one has ever made me come the way that you do, Stella," I tell her honestly, my fingertips creeping closer to her ass. "And no woman has ever turned me on this badly either. You drive me wild."

When my finger slides further, just barely pressing against her asshole, she moans and begins to ride my dick. Her eyes burrow into mine, but it's not like she's searching for something. Instead, it's like we're talking without having to say a fucking word. I feel her in every single place in my body right now. And in this moment, with her rocking back and forth on my cock and her hazel eyes looking into mine, I feel like she's a part of me now.

I'm scared she always will be too.

"Ridge …" My name comes from her plump lips in a weak whisper just as tears spring into her eyes. She doesn't say anything else; she doesn't need to either.

We both know that this is the end of the road for us, and as I play with the edge of her ass, I swallow thickly.

"Right here, baby. Take it," I utter. "Take every inch because until you're gone, it's all yours."

Her fingernails dig into my shoulders, damn near drawing blood, and she bounces herself harder on my cock, taking what she needs from me while she still can.

She doesn't need to tell me she's coming because I feel her pussy begin to quiver for me. And when she cries out my name, cum shoots from my cock, filling her full, just like I wish I could every single day for the rest of my life.

Her body continues to rock against mine, though it gets slower and slower. And when she leans forward, burying her face into my neck, I know that right then is probably the last time I'll be that close to Stella Stewart.

And I know there's not a single fucking woman who's going to fill the void she's going to leave me with.

Chapter 22

Ridge

WE'RE BACK FROM THE BOAT RIDE, AND STELLA HAS disappeared down the hallway to pack her things. She's been quiet ever since we finished fucking on my boat, and it's clear that she's pulling away from me before she's even actually gone. I can feel her growing more distant, putting space between us like nothing ever happened.

No matter how much I loved showing her the lighthouse and taking her on my boat, it doesn't change the fact that, in a few hours, I have to drive her to the airport so she can leave Maine and go back to New York. Whatever the hell this thing between us is, it's coming to an end, and there's nothing I can do to stop that.

I lean forward on my couch to give Marlin a pat on the stomach while he lies on the floor at my feet. He rolls onto his back, snorting a few times, and I chuckle, shaking my head just before I hear the rolling wheels on a suitcase.

I sit up, and my gaze finds Stella. But when I look at her, she does everything in her power to look anywhere besides at me.

When I stand up, my eyes take in the tote bag slung on her shoulder—as if she's heading out the door right now. On her feet are the same fancy boots that she arrived in.

I narrow my eyes. "I thought we didn't need to leave for another hour?"

She stops, and her brows pull together slightly as her eyes grow misty. "Ridge, I called a taxi." She keeps her gaze away from my eyes. "I think we both know this will be a lot easier if we cut things off right now rather than do the whole thing ... where you take me to the airport and give me a hug and a kiss and we pretend like we'll never hear from each other again."

"Would it really be that bad if we did?" I throw my arms out. "Are you that against anything going further? What is it? Are you too good for a small town in Maine? Or are you too good for a lobster fisherman from that small town?"

"You're really going to say that to me?" she hisses through gritted teeth, her eyes finally finding mine, glaring into them. "After everything I told you about my upbringing, you truly think that I think I'm too good?"

I take a step toward her, keeping my fists balled at my sides. She gets under my skin. She has ever since I was working on my boat and she showed up at the wharf with her iPad tucked under her arm, trying to sell me and my father on something her company had convinced her we'd want. And now, she's not just under my skin; she's in every fucking part of me, and I don't think I'll ever get rid of her.

I stop when I'm half a foot away and stare down at her. "I don't know what I think, Stella. You're fucking impossible to figure out. One minute, you're a bitch. The next, you're sweet. Then you're funny. Suddenly, you're as cold as the fucking ice outside." I shrug. "I don't know what to fucking make of you because you are the most complicated creature I have ever met."

She fights a sniffle before quickly wiping her eyes with the back of her hand.

"What would you prefer I do, Ridge?" she whispers with her lips trembling. "Tell my boss to fuck off? Stay here and hope that it works out with a man I met two weeks ago?" Looking down, she wipes her eyes once more. "This isn't a fairy tale, Ridge. Or a Hallmark movie. It's real life." Hazel eyes flash back to mine. "And in real life, people can't just give everything up because they have feelings for someone. Especially not when they've worked so hard to get to where they are. They can't just throw all caution to the wind just for a few feelings."

"I didn't ask you to give everything up," I say, shaking my head. "We could both travel to see each other. We can text. Jesus Christ, at least fucking think about this."

Inhaling a shaky breath, she chews her lip nervously to stop it from quivering. "I'm sorry I tried to get your family to sell your land. One thing I've learned since being here is that this land … this entire place … it's not just a piece of the earth that you own." She smiles sadly. "It's a part of all of you. It's what makes your family who they are. I'm so sorry I ever tried to take that away." She breathes out a miserable laugh. "I'm sorry I ever thought I could."

Taking a step forward, she stands on her tippy-toes and brushes her lips against mine.

"I had the best Christmas with your family, Ridge Adams." She kisses me before sinking back down onto flat feet. "I hope you never take them for granted because a group like yours?" She sniffles. "I would kill for a family like that."

"Stella, just wait," I whisper. "Please. Just let me take you to the airport. We can talk on the way."

"What's the point?" More tears fall, and she gives me the tiniest, saddest smile. "Goodbye, Ridge."

As she walks away from me, I don't know what it is or why ... but I stand there, frozen.

Unable to speak.

Unable to yell.

And unable to run after her when the sound of a car pulls up and takes her away.

Stella

Pain shoots through my chest, radiating deeper inside of me and threatening to make me break down. I know I'm pathetic for feeling this way. I haven't known this man long enough to experience these deep feelings. There's so much about him that I have yet to find out. He could be the worst human on the planet, and I wouldn't know it yet because we haven't spent enough time together.

And yet here I am, driving away from his house in the back seat of a taxi. Running away while I still have a little bit of composure to do so.

For too long, I wasn't in control of my own life. Now, I'm independent. I've proven to myself that I can make it on my own with no parents, no family. And only a few friends because before anyone gets close, I sabotage the relationship and push them away. That way, they can't leave me first.

In the end, I know this is for the best. My whole life is in the city, and long-distance relationships only work when you have a goal in mind. What would our goal even be? We both like where we live and don't want to leave.

Folding my arms across my chest, I hug myself tightly as I wedge my body against the seat of the car. There's always been someone I could depend on to comfort me when things got rough.

Me. Because I'm the one person who can't leave.

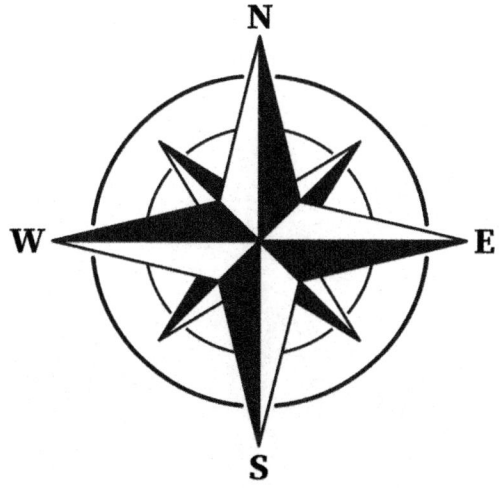

Chapter 23

Ridge

As I walk up the hill toward my truck, Jake and Connor quickly speed away from the small parking lot next to the bait shed, toward the driveway. Neither one of them was very excited to haul on New Year's Eve, but we needed to get out to get all of our gear hauled through before the weather gets shitty in a few days.

I think once they realized they could go out tonight and get drunk and sleep in on New Year's Day, they were okay with it. But this morning? Those two were miserable. Then again, I've been miserable for four days now. Ever since that damn city girl took off, taking my heart right along with her.

I get into my truck and start the engine, quickly cranking the heat up because it's been sitting here since three thirty this morning and it's fucking freezing in here. It's something I do even though I know it's stupid because my house is up the hill, about a quarter mile away. So, it'll never warm up in here by the time I get there. But oh well. It makes me feel better.

Backing out of my parking spot, I drive away from the small parking lot at the wharf and toward my house. And as I turn down my driveway, my eyes narrow when I see my mom's SUV parked in front of my garage.

"What's she doing here?" I mutter.

It's not that uncommon for her to swing by and let Marlin out, but normally not this late in the day when she knows I'll be home soon.

Quickly getting out of the cold truck, I close the door and grab my lunch box from the back before heading inside. As I'm sliding my boots off, the sound of Marlin's feet and his snorting has me smiling because no matter how long of a day it was, that guy is always excited to see me.

"Hey, hon," my mom calls, and when I walk into the living room, she's sitting on the couch. "Hope you don't mind. I stopped in to check on Marlin, and he seemed a bit sad, so I stayed with him and watched TV."

"I don't care," I say, giving her a small smile.

Plopping down on the couch, I'm aware that I smell like bait, but I don't have enough life in me right now to rush to the shower.

"How'd they look out there today?" she asks, patting Marlin's head when he jumps back up onto the couch and curls up beside her. "Any lobsters out there?"

"Not many—that's for sure," I reply. "Hopefully, they pick up soon."

"At least the price is good." She winks. "I would know because it went up this morning, and the other fisherman were pretty impressed."

"When the price is that good, it means there's not shit for lobsters out there." I sigh, reclining back. "Oh well though. We're making a paycheck. That's what matters."

"Exactly." She pauses, and I know right away that she's going to bring up something I don't want to talk about. I don't know what it is, but the way she searches my face, I know it's something bad. "Baby, you've seemed pretty off the past few days. Everything all right?"

Taking my phone out, I pretend like I'm scrolling social media. I mean, I guess I'm not pretending. I really am flipping through it, but I'm not actually looking at any of it.

"Yeah, I'm fine." I keep my voice level and unaffected.

"Okay," she whispers. "It's just ... ever since a certain girl left, your text responses to me have been pretty short. And I've tried to call you a few times, but you don't answer. I know my son. And when something is wrong, this is what you do. You hide."

She's not wrong. I have been avoiding her. I've been avoiding everyone, aside from the two guys who work for me because they aren't going to ask me about Stella. My brothers? They all have, and I'm tired of hearing her name.

"I hardly know her, Mom." The words come out more defensively than I planned them to, so I quickly try to smooth it over. "I mean, she was only here for two weeks. So ... why would I care that she left?"

"And in those two weeks, she spent more time with you than anyone else, Ridge." She points out the obvious. "I could see the way you looked at her, baby. It's all right to admit you liked the girl. It won't make you less of a man, FYI." She giggles. "In fact, it's kind of manly to admit you like someone, if you ask me."

"I gotta go take a shower. I smell," I grumble, standing up, but of course, she stands up too.

"Ridge, I don't know what's going on with you, but if it has anything to do with Stella, you need to put your pride aside and figure out how to make it better."

I don't look at her, but I can hear the worry in her voice.

"And for what it's worth, I've known you your entire life, and I've never seen you look at anyone the way you looked at that girl," she whispers. "And guess what. She looked at you the same way right back."

I don't say anything back to my mom because I don't know what I'd even say. But even she's tired of my shit because a moment later, she leaves.

For days, I keep going back and forth between two thoughts.

One, I hardly knew Stella, and it's stupid that I care this much.

And two, what if she was … my person or whatever, and I let her go? And now, she's going to find someone else. Someone who is much more sophisticated than I will ever be.

I walk into the bathroom and start the shower, letting it get scorching hot because I froze my ass off the entire day. Just like every other day since she left, I know, within seconds, my eyes will shut, and I'll be stroking my cock to memories of her.

But when I step into the shower, I realize something.

My mom is right. I have never looked at anyone the way I looked at Stella. And it doesn't matter if I've known her ten minutes, ten days, or ten years. I can't ignore that feeling I've had since the first night we spent together.

Maybe she's back in the city, knowing that's where she belongs and not even thinking about me. But if I never talk to her again, in person …

How will I know for sure?

Quickly, I wash my hair and my body and turn the shower off.

I don't know what a simple man like me will do in New York City, on probably the busiest night of the entire year there, but that doesn't matter. I've got a fucking flight to book. And if I can catch one soon, I can be there to kiss her at midnight.

Stella

Another flight with another older man.

I keep my headphones off because this time, the older man beside me isn't annoying me like the one did the last time I took this same flight to Maine, even though the man from weeks ago talked less than this one today. The difference is, I'm not being a complete bitch to him. In fact, he's helped the flight pass quickly.

"So, this friend you're going to see," he asks, looking over at me through his thick glasses, "does he know you're coming?"

"No," I say, cringing slightly.

I have the cold sweats because I'm so incredibly nervous. We're landing soon, and I don't even have a plan—well, other than drive to Holiday Harbor and talk to Ridge. This seems crazy, like something out of one of those stupid Hallmark movies that I hate so much. But this morning, when I woke up, I knew that I wasn't ready for things to end with Ridge. At least not until we have a real conversation.

Reaching over, he pats my knee. "I'm sure it'll make his whole day. I know it would make mine if I was a younger fellow and a pretty girl caught a flight on New Year's Eve just to give me a smooch at midnight."

My mouth hangs open. "George!" I laugh. "I didn't say anything about kissing him at New Year's! I don't even know if he'll be home." I grimace. "He could be out at a … you know … a party. Probably planning on kissing someone else at midnight. Who knows?"

"Eh, you didn't have to say anything," he returns, grinning like a fool. "And I doubt anyone he's kissing is as pretty as you, dear."

I chew my lip feverishly.

Suddenly, my plan seems stupid, and I'm not sure what I was even thinking. Ridge is an attractive, single man. Why would he be home alone on New Year's Eve? And what's worse is, when I get to his house, it'll be nearly nine o'clock at night.

God knows what he'll be doing by that time on New Year's Eve.

A few minutes ago, the captain came over the radio and said we had started our descent. With the shifting of the airplane and the lights out the window getting closer to us, I know soon, we'll be landing.

If I was smart, I'd probably call him first. Or just come to my senses and catch a flight right back to New York when this plane turns around to go there.

"Here we go," George mumbles, bracing the armrests, just like he did during takeoff.

Looking out the window, I wait anxiously because any second ... we're going to land. And while everyone else is scared of landings, I'm not. For me, it's when I can finally breathe again.

I walk slowly next to George as we make our way up the ramp.

"I hope you have a great visit with your brother, George." I smile, but when his face grows somber, my heart sinks a little.

"Thanks, kiddo. The truth is, my brother passed away last week, and I'm here for his funeral." His eyes crinkle further at the sides. "Guess I didn't want that look of sympathy if I told you that right at takeoff. And plus, I figured if I lied, it would make me feel like I really was going to see my brother."

Just before we reach the inside of the airport, he takes my hand. "You're young, kid. But guess what. You blink, and you'll be an old geezer like me, traveling more for funerals than you do anything else." He squeezes my hand. "Tell this friend of yours how you feel. Take the chance."

Through the tears in my eyes, I shrug. "How'd you know that's what I came here for? I told you I was coming to see a friend."

"Because I'm ancient, my dear. I can spot a fool in love anywhere." And then he drops my hand and begins shuffling out the door.

And I'm so lost in my thoughts as his words replay in my brain; I almost feel like I'm dreaming when I walk into the lobby and Ridge is sitting in a chair, looking down at his phone on the other side of the rope.

For the outgoing flight to New York.

For a second, I stare at him, wondering if he's really there or if I'm dreaming.

"Ma'am, you can't stand here. You need to keep walking until you're past that sign up there," an older woman barks at me, and still, I'm too dumbfounded.

"Ma'am, I said—" she starts again.

But I can't hear her anymore because the second his eyes find me, he shares the same *are you really here* expression that I'm certain is painted on my face.

And it wouldn't matter what else was going on in this airport; I wouldn't be able to see it because right now, it's just me and Ridge.

Well, it is until the TSA agent is directly next to me. Now yelling into my ear. "Ma'am! I said—"

"I'm … I'm going to move," I whisper to her, keeping my eyes on Ridge. "Just give me a second."

Standing up, he walks to the rope and stops just in front of me. "What are you doing here, city girl?" He looks me up and down, like he still can't believe I'm in Maine.

Tears blur my vision, and I sniffle through a smile. "Well … I hope it's the same thing you're doing—why you're waiting for a flight to New York," I croak out, thankful that the woman has moved on to yelling at someone else so that we can have this moment. "I came here to see you."

He's silent for a beat or two before finally tilting his head to the side. "I was headed to New York to find some redheaded beauty who's as sweet as she is salty. Was hoping to kiss her at midnight." Reaching over to me, he cups my cheeks. "Looks like you saved me the trip."

Tears stream down my cheeks, but right when I open my mouth to speak, the lady is back.

"I said, you cannot—"

Stepping over the rope, Ridge grabs my hand and pulls me behind him. "Don't worry," he calls over his shoulder. "I'll get her out of the way."

I follow closely behind him, giggling through my tears as he rushes us out into the lobby of the small airport. Once we're there, he stops and turns toward me.

"You came back," he whispers. "You really fucking came back."

"I did." I wrap my arms around his abdomen and tilt my chin up. "I had to."

"Me too," he answers. "I didn't know how the hell I was going to find my way around in the city, but I needed to find you."

"You didn't have plans?" I ask, chewing my lip. "You know, it is New Year's Eve and all."

A mischievous smirk tugs at his lips, and he bends his head down closer to mine. "Fireball, before my dumbass realized I was stupid to let you leave, the only plans I had for New Year's was stroking my cock while thinking about you." His chin lifts, and he watches my breathing grow heavier as I imagine him pleasuring himself to thoughts of me.

"And now that you're here, I won't have to fuck my own hand. Because I'll be deep inside your pussy instead. All fucking night. That way, I can show you how much I've missed you."

I clench my legs together. It's a lame attempt to lessen the ache between my thighs, and my heart beats faster when he grips my chin.

"What do you say, New York? Want to ring in the new year while you're riding my cock?"

"Yes." I barely choke out the three-letter word. "Let's go to your house." I step back and pull his hand. "Now."

He follows behind, his fingers caressing mine, but when we get outside, I let him lead me to his truck. Quickly, he opens the passenger door, but instead of closing it, he leans his body against me, kissing me fast and hard.

"We're not going to my house, baby. That's too far for me to wait. And besides, my mom is watching Marlin because I'm supposed to be headed to New York." He kisses me again. "I'm taking you to the closest motel, Stell. Because I can't wait any longer than that to stick my dick inside of you. Especially when I know you're fucking soaked right now, aren't you, baby?"

I squirm in my seat, nodding quickly. "Yes," I whimper.

Reaching between my legs, he nestles his hand against the fabric of my leggings. "Fuck, I can feel the heat pumping out of you," he growls, grinding his hand across and making me whimper. "I promise, I'm going to take care of you."

"Ridge," I moan. "Yes. I need more ..."

Rubbing the pad of his thumb in circles, he kisses me once more. "Soon, baby. So soon. Hang tight. I'll have that pussy filled in no time."

When he steps back, I whimper when his hand leaves from between my thighs. He shuts the door and jogs around to the other side. My mind is going crazy, and the only thing that can calm it . . .

Is being close to this man.

We have a lot of talking to do, but before we can do that, I need to be closer to him than ever.

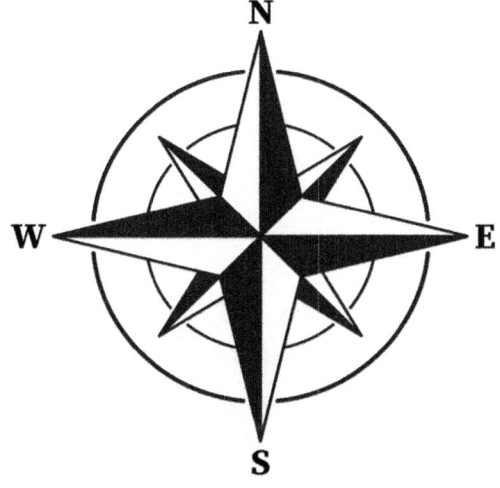

Chapter 24

Ridge

IN THE ELEVATOR, I PULL HER BACK TO ME AND GRIND MY HARD COCK against her ass. "Feel that?" I say into her ear before pulling her earlobe with my teeth.

Taking my hand, she pulls it to the front of her, sliding it between her legs. Her greedy, hot pussy rubs against my palm, and she whimpers, "I can't wait any longer."

I look around, not seeing a camera anywhere—and truthfully not fucking caring if there is one. I move my palm upward, edging it against the band of her leggings before sliding it under the fabric.

"Dirty fucking girl," I hiss. "No panties again?"

I curl my finger, rubbing it against her clit and loving the heat that's pumping from her body. I slip one finger inside of her, and she soaks me, making me wish it were my tongue inside of her instead.

Sliding her hand down, she reaches between us, rubbing her palm back and forth against my cock. Even through my jeans, the friction drives me mad because I've missed her so fucking much.

The elevator reaches our floor, and just before the doors open, I slide my hand from her leggings. But before she can leave, I grip her chin with my other hand and force her to look at me.

"Open up that slutty mouth that I've missed so much," I say gruffly. "Taste yourself."

As she does what she was told, I slip my finger between her plump lips. The elevator doors open, but from the corner of my eye, I don't see anyone—thankfully.

"Suck, baby. Lick my finger clean."

Her lips work the length of my finger, making more blood rush to my cock, and I swallow back a groan.

"Good girl," I whisper, slowly pulling my finger from her mouth. "Soon, you'll be tasting my dick too. And I think you're going to love how we taste together."

Before the doors have a chance to close, I lead us out and toward our room. My cock isn't even inside of her yet, and it's pulsating. I need her so badly. And soon, she'll be all mine.

I keep my hand tightly around hers, stopping at our room number and trying not to fumble the key. I barely get the door open, and her jacket is off, and she's pushing me inside, kissing me like a wild animal.

I reach between us, tearing her leggings down and yanking her shoes off. I pull her shirt over her head, leaving her only in her bra before I lift her up and walk her toward the bed. Setting her down, I kiss her again before slowly working my way down her body. I wrap my forearms around her thighs and yank her until my mouth is on her heat.

And, goddamn, I missed that fucking taste.

When I drive my tongue inside of her tightness, her fingers wrap around pieces of my hair, and she pulls on it while she watches me intensively.

"Fuck ... yes," she chokes out. "I missed your mouth."

I don't answer because I'm enjoying having my tongue buried in her pussy right now. Sliding my palm up, I rest it on her stomach while I lift her a little higher so that even her ass is off the bed. The sounds she's making are driving me fucking wild, and I'm expecting my cock to shoot off at any second, but I try to keep myself contained.

Just as her hips begin to buck against my face and I know she's close, I pull away, which instantly earns me a pout. I waste no time giving answers though, and instead, I flip her onto her stomach, flat on the bed. And force her knees under her and her ass in the air.

Crawling on to the edge of the bed, I grip her hips roughly, scraping my fingertips into her flesh before I push my face against her ass. Greedily, my tongue drives a little deeper inside of her before I work my way toward her tight pussy, angling her slightly upward for a better taste before moving back to her ass.

I drop one hand down, bringing it between her legs and shoving a finger deep into her heat while I continue to eat her ass the way I've wanted to since I first saw how fucking hot it was.

"Ridge," she says in a whiny yet desperate tone, pushing back against me. "Oh my ... fucking God."

"I need to make you mine, baby," I taste her once more, sliding my tongue back to her pussy before I pull away and flip her onto her back.

Moving over her, I lift one of her legs high before sliding my cock into her heat. Her eyebrows knit together, and her mouth hangs open as a sob escapes her lips.

"I've missed you," she cries as I thrust into her harder. Her hands fall to my back, and her nails press into my flesh. "I've missed you so fucking much."

Bringing my lips to hers, I kiss her before I release my hold on her leg. "I've missed everything about you, Fireball." My words hardly come out in a rasp, and I thrust in and out of her. "I can't tell you how many times I've stroked my cock, just wishing it were you." I kiss her again. "I knew no one was ever going to come close."

Our eyes melt into each other's, and yet we don't say a fucking word while I bury myself deeper and deeper inside of her. We don't need to because, right now, the only thing that matters is, she's here. With me.

She's here . . . in Maine.

"You feel so good, baby." I take one of her hands from my back and push it into the mattress.

This isn't the first time we've had sex, and yet I've never felt this close to her before. I don't know if I've ever felt this close to another human being—ever. Her hazel eyes stare into mine, and as corny as it sounds, this really doesn't feel like fucking. It feels like something more.

We've barely begun, and yet I already feel like I can't hold it much longer before I fucking blow. It's like she knows what I'm feeling because her legs wrap around my waist, and she shifts her hips forward and back, creating more friction.

"I'm so close," she whispers, dragging in a shaky breath. "I want you to come with me."

"Say the word, baby. Tell me when, and I'll fill you up, just like I've been imagining doing for days." I push her hand harder to the mattress when her nails press into my back.

My balls begin to draw up, and I pray she says the fucking word soon. Like she's reading my mind, she whimpers, her mouth falling open.

"Now," rushes from her lips in a squeak just as her pussy begins to strangle my cock. "Right now . . ." she cries out louder.

As much as I want to stare into her eyes while I fill her, making her mine, I bury my face into her neck while my hips continue to thrust, and her moans fill our room. And when we both finally stop thrusting against each other, a shiver runs down my body before I pull back and look down at her.

"Fuck, I missed you," I whisper roughly before I flip us both over so that she's on top.

Keeping my cock still inside of her, I grip her hips. Because we have a lot of lost time to make up for, and I plan to spend it being as close to this woman as fucking possible.

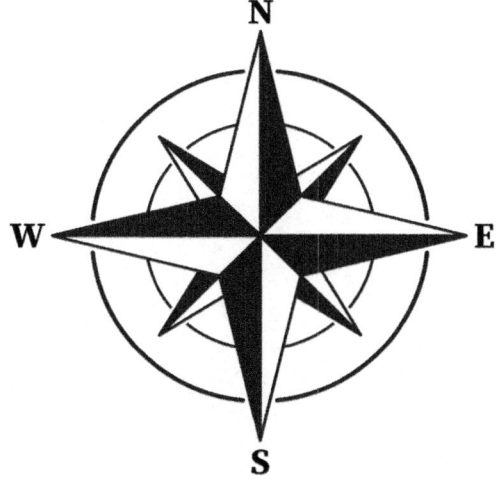

Chapter 25

Stella

RIDGE KEEPS HIS LIPS AGAINST MY HAIR, HOLDING ME CLOSE TO his naked body, yet I still cling to him like it's not close enough.

"So," his deep voice drawls through the hotel room, "what does this mean? Where does this leave us, Stella?"

I knew this was coming, but unlike last time, when I wanted to out-run any questions, now ... I'm not scared. I know things aren't going to be easy, and I know we don't have all the answers right now and we won't for a long time, but I'm positive when it comes to one thing: I want this man in my life.

"I don't really know," I say honestly. "I just know that no matter how much this thing between us might not make sense, I still am not ready for it to end." I crane my neck a bit more, kissing his side. "In fact, it's the op-posite. I want to see where it goes." My cheeks heat up, and I bury my face into his side. "I mean ... if you want that too. Maybe that seems too sudd—"

"Stop rambling," he commands before he tugs at my hand. "Hey, look at me, would you?"

When he continues tugging on me, reluctantly, I roll onto my stom-ach and peek up at him. "Yes?" I utter, afraid I'm going to scare him away with what I just said.

I mean, we clearly have great sex. Maybe that's all he was going to New York for. That's a bit of an expensive booty call, if you ask me, but he would have also gotten to see Times Square during New Year's, so maybe it would have been worth it.

He strokes my cheek, sitting upward and pressing his back against the headboard. "I've been one grumpy dick since you left. Just ask my crew to-day. I'm lucky they didn't quit." He chuckles lightly. "Stella, I don't know where this is going either. Hell, I'm not even sure how this is going to work. All I know is, I'm a man who doesn't even chase a girl across town to get her attention. And you had me willing to go to New York fucking City, just to see you again."

I bite my bottom lip to prevent myself from looking like a complete loser with the cheesy smile that so badly wants to spread across my lips. Trying to keep my composure, I swallow. "So then, you're feeling it too?"

"Fireball, I felt it that day at the tree farm when, for the first time, you actually let me see the real you." His words are so gentle, despite his deep voice. "You got under my skin from day one, but now ... you're in my fucking soul too. And I'm just a lobster fisherman from Maine, Stella. This isn't shit I've ever felt, much less said out loud."

"Your family though"—I cringe—"they probably don't want me coming back. I mean, considering how we all met in the first place."

He doesn't even flinch. He simply tosses back, "My mom was waiting for me at my house when I got in from haul today. Pretty much telling me I shouldn't have let you go." His thumb drags against my bottom lip. "My family likes you—I promise you that much."

"I quit my job." I blurt the words out for the first time since I told Victor I was done a few days ago. "It just didn't seem like me anymore."

I expect him to seem surprised, but he tilts his head to the side thoughtfully.

"I hope I didn't bring you to do that. I know your career means a lot to you."

I can't explain to him why I quit because no matter how I spin it, he is the reason why I decided to walk away. So, even though I'll probably be terrible at explaining myself, I try anyway.

"By spending time with your family and exploring where you're from— even going out on your boat, Ridge ..." My heart swells bigger with each word. "You showed me what's important. It's not climbing a stupid, impossible ladder at a job I'm not passionate about. Or overdeveloping land into something chaotic instead of beautiful just to make a buck." I rest my hand on his chest. "You are so proud of everything your family has built. And of yourself too. I want to have that too." I shrug sadly. "I guess I got so lost in wanting to rely only on myself that I lost sight of everything else."

After searching my face for a moment or two without speaking, Ridge suddenly grabs my waist and pulls me on top of him before forcing our lips together.

"I'm so fucking glad you're here," he says against my lips before kissing me again. "Happy New Year, Stella."

I pull back, looking at the clock on the nightstand that reads twelve o'clock before I glance back at him. "Happy New Year, Outlaw."

And as I lean down and kiss him again and his cock grows hard against my ass, I know that, hands down, this man has given me the best Christmas ever and now the best New Year's Eve too. And seeing as he booked this motel room for a few days, I'd say New Year's Day will be another record-breaking holiday for me.

Chapter 26

Stella

"ARE YOU SURE NO ONE IS GOING TO FIND IT WEIRD THAT I'M here?" I whisper, gripping Ridge's arm tighter as we walk into his grandparents' house.

It's his grandfather's birthday on his mother's side, and I sort of feel rude, being here, but he said he wouldn't come without me, so here I am.

"They'll be excited and probably ask you when our wedding is," he says, laughing. But he quickly cringes and looks at me. "I'm actually fucking serious, so promise me it won't weird you out and then you run away again."

I pat his abdomen with my other hand. "I'm not going to run away, big guy. You can calm down." I look around the old but adorable house. "Wow, this house is so ..."

"Old?" he guesses, looking around. "Was it the wallpaper that gave it away? Or that smell? I'm not quite sure what it actually is, but it screams ancient."

"Hey now, that's not nice to say about your grandparents," Katherine says, walking around the corner toward us. She smiles when she sees me. "Stella, it's nice to see you back in Maine."

When she hugs us each, one at a time, Ridge shrugs. "For the record, I wasn't talking about Grammy and Grampy. I was talking about their house." He looks around, sniffing. "And if you try to say it doesn't smell in here, you're a liar, *Katherine*. So, don't bother."

"Don't call me Katherine, you jerk; you know I hate that." His mom swats at him and rolls her eyes. "Fine, my rotten child. It smells in here. This house was built over a hundred years ago, so of course it smells. Everything smells when it's old—even people." She narrows her eyes. "One day, your dad and I will smell, too, and you'll have to take care of us."

"I'll pass," Ridge utters. "I have three brothers who are much nicer than I am. They'll do a great job."

His mom, being used to his sense of humor, laughs before she throws her arm around me. "Come on, guys. We were just about to eat."

I've been in Maine for three days now. But for the first two, we hardly left the motel room. And then, yesterday, when we finally did get to Ridge's house, we watched movies with Marlin and did absolutely nothing.

"Do you know how long you're staying this time?" she asks, leading us down the hallway, where I hear laughter and chatter.

"No, not yet," I answer softly, unsure of what to say because there's no way I'm just going to stay here forever with a man I haven't even known a month. I'm also not going to say that I never want to move here because it's been crossing my mind more and more. But I don't want to rush things.

And before I drop everything and give up my apartment in New York, first, we need to properly date. Even if a lot of it will be done long distance.

"Well, please come by and visit before you go back." She cringes. "Good luck. Just so you know, my family is loud. All of them."

And then we're walking into the dining room, and every single eye at the table ... is on me. Just as my heart begins to race and my palms grow sweaty, Ridge squeezes my hand.

"Wow, your hand's gross," he whispers into my ear, chuckling. "Good thing you're hot. That would be a major turnoff."

I roll my eyes at him but refrain from hitting him in front of his family. And as he turns toward everyone and starts to introduce me, I realize what a big step this is. Being here, with not only his brothers and parents, but his aunts, uncles, and cousins too.

"Hey, everyone. This is my girlfriend, Stella." He smirks, his eyes twinkling at me because he just called me his freaking girlfriend for the first time in front of a room full of people. "And, Stella, this is everyone."

Once everybody waves and says hello from their seats, Riley struts over toward us.

On his lips is his usual grin, and he throws his arm around me. "Oh, hey, city girl. You here to try to buy out my grandparents' house for that fancy company you work for?" He looks around. "Just a heads-up, there's about ... four or five layers of wallpaper caked on these walls."

"Har-har," I say, rolling my eyes. "My days of buying property for Ironbound are over." I glance at the wall. "And to be honest, I kinda think the wallpaper is charming."

He seems stunned, and yet, somehow, he still looks amused and play-ful. I think that expression may permanently stay on his face though.

"Does that mean you left the city and are back in Holiday Harbor for good?" He lifts a brow. "After all, this guy did call you his girlfriend."

I side-eye Ridge before I nudge him with my shoulder. "He did choose a very public moment to do that, didn't he?" I grumble. "And, no, I'm not moving here just yet."

Riley covers his mouth and then drops his hands down and claps. "Not yet?" He slaps his big brother on the shoulder. "She said not yet, bro. Not *never*. Or not … *no way*. She said—and I quote—'not yet.'"

After clapping his hands a few more times, he turns away and heads back to his seat, leaving me the perfect chance to look at my apparently new boyfriend and hit him with a questioning gaze.

"Girlfriend, huh?"

He dips his lips closer to my ear. "Not moving to Holiday Harbor yet, huh?" He pulls back, winking. "I like the sound of that, Fireball. Because you didn't say never. You said yet. And, yeah, you heard what I said. Girlfriend." His eyes dance. "What do you have to say about that?"

Turning my body toward him, I gaze up. "I'd say … all right, boyfriend. Let's go eat, shall we?"

"Oh, by the end of the night, I'll be eating more than just the food on the table," he drawls. "But, yes, babe, let's eat. I'm starving."

We walk toward a table full of people I don't know, and something that would have terrified me a month ago suddenly doesn't seem so bad. Because the guy next to me? Wherever he is, that's where I want to be too.

Chapter 27

Stella

Six Months Later

I LOOK AROUND THE APARTMENT THAT HAS BEEN MY HOME FOR almost three years now, and I'm not even sure what this feeling inside of me is. This place took so much blood, sweat, and tears for me to have, and now, I'm letting it go. On one hand, I can't help but wonder if I'm making a mistake, putting all my eggs in Ridge Adams's basket and moving to Maine. I swore I'd never give up my life for anyone, and yet here I am.

But on the other hand, the city just hasn't felt the same since I spent those few weeks in Maine. And now, after going back and visiting Maine a few times, New York really doesn't feel like home any more. I'm not sure that New York was ever my dream, but more maybe a goal that I reached and didn't want to leave behind.

There's a knock on the door, causing me to frown. I know the new tenants are moving in, but they aren't supposed to be here for a few more days, and I'm not sure who else would be coming to see me. The few friends I do have in the city met me for dinner last night, and we said our goodbyes then.

When I look through the peephole, my entire face breaks into a smile when I see who's on the other side of my door, and I can't get it open fast enough.

Just as soon as the door opens, I'm leaping against Ridge, forcing him to catch me and wrapping my legs around his waist.

"You're here!" I squeal, kissing him over and over again—the way annoying girlfriends who haven't seen their boyfriends in three weeks do. "What happened to *I'll see you when you get here, baby*?" I say in my best grumpy Ridge Adams's voice.

Walking us into the apartment, he grins before kissing me back.

"That was never the plan, babe," he drawls. "You're just stubborn, so I had to tell you that to get you to stop insisting that you didn't need help."

"I don't need—" I start to say, but his lips stop me.

Slowly pulling back, he dips his forehead to mine. "I know you don't need help, Stella Stewart. I know you're a strong, independent woman who could have loaded your own damn car up and driven to Maine all by yourself." He kisses me again. "But you have a boyfriend who wants to help. And a boyfriend who isn't catching shit for lobsters right now and needed to take a few days to let his traps set, anyway."

I love when he talks in lobster lingo. And even though, when he's on the phone with a fishing buddy, I don't usually know what they are even saying, I love the way he sounds. And by now, I know "super set" just means he's going to not haul for a few extra days because the lobsters are scarce.

"Okay, so what you're saying is, me allowing you to help me is kinda like I'm doing you a favor." I raise a brow. "So, I'm really helping you avoid feeling like a loser who isn't catching any lobsters."

"Geesh, go easy on me, baby, would you?" he drones. "But yeah. Yeah, that's pretty much it."

"You'll always be a winner to me," I say cheesily before kissing his cheek. "I love you. Thank you for coming to help. Even when I swore I didn't want you to, I did. I'm really glad you're here."

"Love you too, you complicated-as-hell woman, who I love so much," he says, setting me on my feet and looking down at me. "What do you say, Fireball? Time to get the car loaded and head home?"

Home. I've never really felt like I had one, but now … I somehow know that's exactly where I'm headed.

The last time I went to Maine, he walked me around some oceanfront property right next to the wharf. For the first time, he told me he loved me and that he missed me the second I left Maine. And even though he'd lived alone for his entire adult life, his house just didn't feel like a home when I wasn't there.

Everything he said, I felt the same way. And I think I had loved him long before we said the words out loud, too afraid to actually say them. After all, my track record with being lovable really wasn't that strong, and I didn't want to jinx myself.

While we stood next to the water, he told me that even though his family wanted to keep the land in their name, they did want to consider building some sort of educational center for schools to take field trips to. I think Ridge knew that if I was going to move to Maine, it couldn't be just for him. It had to be for something for myself too.

And that's why, next week, we're breaking ground on the Holiday Harbor Educational Center. And I get to be the one to design the building plan, per Ridge's entire family's blessing.

"You all right, beautiful?" he asks, interrupting my thoughts of what a whirlwind my life has been since mid-December.

"Yeah," I whisper.

And as I take one last look around my apartment and walk toward the window to look out at the city, I nod slowly. "It's time."

A little over six months ago, I went to the coast of Maine to seal the deal on a property that I didn't realize was priceless. Instead . . . I brought in the biggest catch of all.

The salty fisherman who wasn't so salty after all.

Acknowledgments

I hope everyone who read Stella and Ridge's story felt a little Christmas magic during the holiday season. Even though, if I had it my way, it would always be Christmas because it's my very favorite time of the year. It's a time where everything just seems a little more peaceful, even in the midst of the chaos, which literally makes no sense. But I understand not everyone has perfect holiday stories, and for those that don't, I hope, one day, the Christmas magic finds you because we all deserve to feel it.

I want to say thank you to my husband, who is the saltiest lobster fisherman of them all. Through all the seasons, you get your boots on and head out into the dangerous, unforgiving sea to earn money to provide for your family. It isn't always a glamorous job, and it sure has trying times, but I also know how much you love and respect the Atlantic. And just like Ridge Adams, it's a part of you. May you always stay safe out there, my love.

Thank you to my entire fishing family, which ranges from my late grandfather to my father-in-law, brother-in-law, uncles, my brother, my cousins, and even my mom, who went on the boat with her dad for years. Thank you all for passing down a love for working hard on the ocean and having a deep respect for all of the creatures that call it home.

Thank you, Maddy McDermot, for keeping the Hannah Gray brand afloat. You are the most incredible PA, and I am so lucky to have you. Love you lots!

Thank you to my bestie, C.L. Rose. She gets stuck with many voice messages from me daily. Sometimes, I'm venting. Sometimes, I'm yawning, and other times, I just need to talk to my best friend. I am thankful every day that the book world brought you and me together. Love you, babe!

Thank you to my other PA, Maggie Marrero, who remembers the smallest details, places endless orders to make sure my PR is adorable, and who even packs and ships them because she knows that I suck at anything to do with a post office. I love you so much!

Thank you, Tina Otero, who does anything from helping me at signings to alpha- and beta-reading my books, giving me plotting opinions, or sometimes … just bullying people into reading Cam Hardy because she's weirdly obsessed—and I love it. Love you to pieces, woman!

Thank you to my incredibly talented editor, Jovana Shirley, who is the badass owner of Unforeseen Editing. This book was outside of my norm. Thank you for helping me make it perfect. Love and adore you to pieces!

Thank you, Sonia Garrigoux, for the beautiful illustrations for my cover. It is everything I wanted and more! Always a treat to work with you.

Thank you, Sarah Grim Sentz at Enchanting Romance Designs, for not only being the sweetest human, but for also being so damn talented. You always help me to make my covers perfect. Thank you for doing the typography and final touches on *The Christmas Catch*.

Thank you, Stacey Blake, for working your magic on another one of my book babies, and making the inside of it look gorgeous with your formatting skills! It's always an honor working with you.

Thank you, once again, to Jaimie Davidson, for being an extra set of eyes and looking through the book for me. You are a true Godsend! Love you!

Thank you, Mackenzie Spruill, for not just being great at being a content creator and managing my TikTok account, but for also being such a huge support system for me and so many other authors. We're all very lucky to have you. Thanks for sticking with me. Love you forever!

Thank you so much to the Smuthood team. You were so patient with me (and my five hundred questions) I can't wait to continue working together in the future!

Special shout-out to my content team for being so freaking amazing! Every single day that I look at social media, I am continuously blown away by the love and support you all show me. I love your words, your graphics, and your vibes. I am truly the luckiest girl to have all of you on my team. I adore each of you beyond words.

And last, but certainly not least, thank you to my readers. Some of you may be new while others have been with me for a while now. No matter where you are in your Hannah Gray journey, just know that I am so thankful you are here. Thank you for giving my words a shot. I'm truly and deeply and forever grateful for you.

Other Books by
HANNAH GRAY

NE University Series
Chasing Sunshine
Seeing Red
Losing Memphis
Read it now!

Brooks University Series
Love, Ally
Forget Me, Sloane
Hate You, Henley
Head to the Brooks University football-verse!

Florida East University
Playing Dane
Stealing Bama
Catching Kye
Binge the series today!

The Puck Boys of Brooks University
Puck Boy
Broken Boy
Filthy Boy
Chosen Boy
Lost Boy
Perfect Boy
Last Boy
Meet the puck boys now

The New England Bay Sharks

Tell Me Lies

Shoot Your Shot

Fool Me Once

Bite Your Tongue

Wake Me Up

meet your next pro hockey book boyfriend!

Stand-alones

Ruthless

READ THIS DARK MAFIA ROMANCE NOW!"

Holiday Romances

The Christmas Catch

The Holiday Trawl

Book 2 in the Holiday Harbor Series coming November 2026!

About the Author

Hannah Gray spends her days in vacationland, living in a small, quaint town on the coast of Maine. She is an avid reader of contemporary romance and is always in competition with herself to read more books every year.

During the day, she loves on her three perfect-to-her daughters and tries to be the best mom she can be. But once she tucks them in at night—okay, scratch that. Once they fall asleep next to her in her bed—because their bedrooms apparently have monsters in them—she dives into her own fantasy world, staying awake well into the late-night hours, typing away stories about her characters. As much as she loves being a wife and mom—and she certainly does love it—reading and writing are her outlet, giving her a place to travel far away while still physically being with her family.

She married her better half in 2013, and he's been putting up with her craziness every day since. As her anchor, he's her one constant in this insane, forever-changing world.

Printed in Dunstable, United Kingdom